"I'm not here to make your life difficult…"

Colt leaned back in his chair and studied Holly's face. "You're still beautiful."

Of course he would go there. That was his way of dealing with life. He charmed. He complimented.

He didn't mean it.

"Don't. I don't want compliments and I don't want you trying to take me down rabbit trails. You're obviously here on business. So why don't we cut to the chase."

He didn't smile. "Of course, right to the point. I'm not here about the café."

Raising her arm, she made a show of checking the time on her watch. "I do have a business to run. Our business. Remember, I send you a check each month."

He shoved himself up from the table and limped to the window. His hand came up to rub the back of his neck.

"Holly, it's about Dixie. That's why I'm here."

Dixie.

The air left the room and her vision darkened. He wasn't here about the café or about them. He was here to tell her something concerning Dixie.

Their daughter.

Brenda Minton lives in the Ozarks with her husband, children, cats, dogs and strays. She is a pastor's wife, Sunday-school teacher, coffee addict and is sleep deprived. Not in that order. Her dream to be an author for Harlequin started somewhere in the pages of a romance novel about a young American woman stranded in a Spanish castle. Her dreams came true, and twenty-plus books later, she is an author hoping to inspire young girls to dream.

Books by Brenda Minton

Love Inspired

Mercy Ranch

Reunited with the Rancher
The Rancher's Christmas Match
Her Oklahoma Rancher
The Rancher's Holiday Hope
The Prodigal Cowboy

Bluebonnet Springs

Second Chance Rancher
The Rancher's Christmas Bride
The Rancher's Secret Child

Martin's Crossing

A Rancher for Christmas
The Rancher Takes a Bride
The Rancher's Second Chance
The Rancher's First Love
Her Rancher Bodyguard
Her Guardian Rancher

Visit the Author Profile page at Harlequin.com for more titles.

The Prodigal
Cowboy

Brenda Minton

LOVE INSPIRED
INSPIRATIONAL ROMANCE

LOVE INSPIRED®
INSPIRATIONAL ROMANCE

Recycling programs
for this product may
not exist in your area.

ISBN-13: 978-1-335-55361-4

The Prodigal Cowboy

Copyright © 2020 by Brenda Minton

This edition published by arrangement with Harlequin Books S.A.

For questions and comments about the quality of this book,
please contact us at CustomerService@Harlequin.com.

Love Inspired
22 Adelaide St. West, 40th Floor
Toronto, Ontario M5H 4E3, Canada
www.Harlequin.com

Printed in U.S.A.

Casting all your care upon him;
for he careth for you.
                —*1 Peter* 5:7

To the caregivers. In taking care of your loved one, find time for yourself.

Chapter One

Colt West rode into town in a Ford truck pulling a two-horse trailer and feeling like he was heading to the hangman's noose. He guessed that was a little dramatic and he wasn't usually given to drama. But when a man came home to face his past, that changed everything. Especially if it meant facing mistakes made and the people he'd hurt. The person he'd hurt.

Hope, Oklahoma. A pretty fanciful name given that the town had been through some hard times. He figured a town struggling to survive needed the moniker more than most. But then, the town didn't need hope; it had Jack West. Colt's father, using the term loosely, had become the town benefactor. He was using the family fortune to rebuild businesses, improve the lives of wounded veterans and lure his children home.

The three of them, Carson, Colt and Daisy, hadn't been too interested in spending time with the one-time abusive alcoholic. But then Carson had fallen prey to the old man, relocating his life and medical practice to Hope and marrying his childhood sweetheart.

And now here was Colt, dragging his broken self back to Hope. He knew it wasn't going to be easy, facing his past for this family reunion. For that reason he'd given himself a goal and a timeline. He was here for at least six weeks, maybe eight. He'd make things right, or at least try. He'd let his body finish healing up from the ugly confrontation with a meaner-than-dirt bull. He'd be in New Mexico and back to his job of bull fighter and sometimes rodeo clown by the end of May.

If Holly Carter didn't kill him.

He headed down Lakeside Drive and spotted the new sign on Mattie's Café. It now read Holly's Café. He slowed and thought about stepping inside that café and what his reception might be. The thought of facing Holly made him want to keep on driving. And he would have done just that if not for the passenger in the back seat of his Ford King Ranch.

Hard as this reunion was going it be, it had to happen.

He turned right at the intersection just past the café and parked next to the building. It was Friday afternoon and the lunch rush hour was long past. No one would mind him parking here, and his horse would be in the shade.

"What are we doing here?" the unhappy voice from the back seat of his truck asked. "I thought we were going to a ranch."

"We have to make a stop first."

"Holly is my birth mom's name." The girl leaned over the seat. She was eleven and a handful. Times ten.

He and Holly had made the best decision they could for their daughter. They'd given Dixie up for adoption. Becky Stafford, a friend of his mother, had spent twenty-five years of her life in the Navy. She hadn't married because her career had taken her around the world. In her late forties, she had found herself retired and yearning for a child. They'd picked her to raise Dixie.

She'd been a strong woman of faith with a lot of love to offer. They could never have managed to give Dixie a stable home life, not at that time in their lives.

"Isn't it?" Dixie pushed, dragging him back to the present.

"Yeah, Holly is your birth mom's name," he answered.

"Is that her café?"

"Yeah, it is."

"You think you're just going to walk in there with me and surprise her? You realize that's not a surprise, it's a heart attack." And at the words *heart attack*, her eyes started to tear up. But she didn't cry. It had been several weeks since Becky passed away and he'd been told she hadn't cried. Not once that anyone knew of. And now, the little things a person said that shouldn't have been difficult had become just that.

He felt the same way.

He wasn't much good at kid stuff, but the girl tearing up as she tried to be strong couldn't be ignored. He patted her arm, awkwardly. "It's going to be okay."

She squinted her eyes and sniffed away the tears. "That's what you say when someone loses a puppy, not a mom."

"You're right about that," he agreed. "I'll learn to do better."

Dixie gave him a steady look, unsure and not too full of hope, and he saw both himself and Holly in her. She had their dark hair, his silver-gray eyes and Holly's sprinkle of freckles across her nose.

"I'm going to hold you to that," she said, as if she knew not to trust him. He wasn't good at keeping promises. Holly knew that better than anyone. Pretty much every woman he'd ever encountered had learned not to put too much stock in his promises.

"Okay. So I'm going in there to talk to Holly. And you're going to wait in the truck."

"In the truck!"

"Because she needs to have this broken to her gently."

"Right, and you're nervous she'll turn us both away."

"Just stay here," he said. It sounded a lot like pleading, but he couldn't help it.

Her expression fell. "Is she going to be upset to see me?"

"Absolutely not," he assured her. "But like you said, we shouldn't spring this on her without some kind of warning."

"You have five minutes," she warned.

"I'm not sure if it's too soon to ground you but I'm sure thinking about it."

She grinned at the warning and he felt as if maybe he'd just done something right as a parent.

"Fine, just leave the truck on. I'm going to finish watching my movie." She sat back, tossed him a look that challenged him to say something and put her feet up on the console between the front seats.

He let it go because he had bigger problems. With a groan, he got out, stretched as much as he possibly could and limped up the sidewalk in the direction of his reckoning. Holly.

For the first of April it was warmer than he'd expected. Or maybe he had a good case of nerves going, because it had been a while since he and Holly had talked. Not that they didn't ever talk, but he wasn't on her list of favorite people. He prepared himself for a less-than-happy reunion.

What he hadn't planned for was his half brother, Isaac West, getting out of his own truck in front of the café. Isaac spotted him and faltered. He yanked off his sunglasses, rubbed his eyes and then slowly pushed his truck door shut.

Colt pretended he hadn't noticed even though he and Isaac both knew better.

Isaac met him on the sidewalk, a half grin on his handsome face. The girls had always liked Isaac. The girls had liked all three West brothers, even before they knew Isaac was a West. And the West brothers had liked the girls.

"Well, well, look what the cat dragged in," Isaac said with a lazy drawl. "You're looking a little worse for wear."

"A broken back will do that for a man."

"Broken back, broken leg and a cracked skull," Isaac corrected. "You got on the business end of that bull."

"But I saved the guy who was under his hooves." Two months later, he was still recuperating from the incident.

"Yeah, you did that." Isaac pulled a toothpick from his pocket and after pulling off the wrapper, stuck it between his teeth. "I didn't expect to see you here."

"I didn't expect to be here. But there are times in a man's life when he realizes he has to come home and make things right."

Isaac's gaze slid to Holly's Café and frowned. "She doesn't need any added pressure."

"I know." Older by a year, Colt didn't need any lectures from his younger brother.

Their dad had been a bounder back in the day. The two of them had gone to the same school and played Little League together and hadn't known they were brothers.

But other people had known. Looking back, he remembered the whispers and knowing looks.

"Then what are you doing, Colt?" Isaac asked.

"I'm hoping I can help."

"You think so, huh?" Isaac peered past him, catching sight of the kid in the car. "Who is that?"

"That?" he mumbled.

"You're going to have to speak up." Isaac turned, giving Colt his good ear, the one not damaged from a head injury sustained in Afghanistan. "And you know who I mean. Who is that sitting in your truck?"

"That's Dixie."

Understanding dawned and Isaac's mouth formed an exaggerated but silent *oh*. "You're going to need some Jesus when you walk through the door of that café."

"You sound like a grandmother," Colt responded.

"Yeah, well, grandmothers have a lot of wisdom." He flashed his dimpled grin. "They also know when to cut tail and run, and when to stay and watch the fire."

Colt adjusted his hat. The movement sent a jolt of pain from his back to his head. He'd been sitting in his truck a little too long. "I don't have much of a choice."

"I know you don't, but this is going to be tough. Holly has a lot going on in her life."

"You think I don't know that?" Colt asked.

Isaac shrugged, chewing on the toothpick. "I reckon you do." His gaze shot past Colt's left shoulder. "Trouble is on the move."

Colt remembered to move slow and steady as he turned. Dixie was out of the truck and heading his way, a backpack over her shoulder and that bent-up straw cowboy hat she liked to wear resting on her head at a cockeyed angle. She wore ripped and faded jeans, a gray T-shirt, worn-out boots and a glare.

"I'm not staying in the truck like some dusty old secret you're trying to hide." She tossed him an old wood cane. "And you might need this, gimpy."

Isaac whistled. "I like her."

Colt leaned on the cane, then counted to ten before answering. "Yeah, me, too. Most of the time."

"You're supposed to be positive and say

life-affirming things so I grow up to have good self-esteem and make smart choices," Dixie said with a grin. Holding her hand out to Isaac, she said, "I'm Dixie West. I just added the West for fun, to make him turn red. I'm really Dixie Stafford."

"I'm your uncle Isaac, and I think you're the best thing that ever happened to him. Would you mind if I give you a hug?"

"Thanks. I doubt he's the best thing that ever happened to me." She grinned big, obviously feeling braver for having Isaac as an ally. She stepped forward and Isaac gave her a hug.

Colt shook his head and gave her a warning look. "You might be right about that, but it doesn't give you the right to talk that way."

Dixie gave him a hard glare but didn't answer.

"So, what's the plan?" Isaac asked.

"We're going in," Dixie told him. She glanced back as she started toward the café. "Come on… Dad."

"I'm gonna…" Colt growled.

"Love her unconditionally," Isaac supplied.

"Yeah, that." Colt took a few steps and glanced back, expecting Dixie to be right behind him.

She wasn't. She might have come out of the truck feeling brave, but now she looked half-scared of what she might find once they stepped into the café.

"You okay?" he asked as she took a step back.

"I think our original plan is best," she told him. "You should break the news to her first. We shouldn't go tromping in there like this and have her faint or something."

"I'll wait out here with her," Isaac offered. "We can get to know each other."

Colt studied the girl facing him with a wild look of fear mixed with bravado. She deserved better than him.

He had a long track record of hurting people.

He was trying to be a better man. He'd been seeking the faith he'd known as a kid, hoping God hadn't given up on him. And he'd been praying hard that his decision—to honor Becky's final request—was the right thing to do.

"Might as well get it over with," Isaac said.

"Yeah, might as well."

He limped up the sidewalk and stepped through the door of the café. His gaze immediately sought her out, watching as she poured coffee for a customer. Her dark hair was pulled back in a ponytail. She'd lost weight since the last time he'd seen her and there were dark circles under her eyes. She was beautiful and always would be. She was also the only woman he'd ever really loved.

Unfortunately, being loved by him hadn't ever done her any good.

As the bells over the door chimed, Holly looked up and her gaze connected with his. She continued to pour coffee until it overflowed the mug, running onto the table and pooling on the floor. The men at the table jumped back, grabbing napkins to mop up the brown liquid.Holly stood frozen, emotions flickering across her face, going from surprised to angry to something undefinable that hit him in the gut, because it looked a lot like pain. The overwhelming emotion that should be tagged to every possible interaction they'd ever had. Pain.

He'd always managed to cause her pain, even now, when he had hoped he was doing the best thing ever for her. Of course, she didn't know that.

Holly saw him enter but she didn't believe it, not at first. It couldn't be Colt, looking rugged but handsome, his hair too long and a few days' growth of whiskers on his too-attractive face as he leaned heavily on a cane and announced his arrival for all the world like she might have been waiting for his return.

"Hey, Holly, you're pouring that coffee all over the table." Martin Finley yanked his hand back from his cup and grabbed the towel off the tray she'd carried over with the coffeepot. "You look like you just saw the nightmare of Christmas past."

"Nothing as good as that," she told him as she took the towel and mopped up the table and then the floor. "More like I saw the Grinch himself."

Her gaze shot back to the man at the door. He'd removed his hat and he pushed a hand through dark hair. For a moment she was eighteen again and a freshman in college, meeting up with a guy she'd known as a child and not realizing the combined power of attraction and loneliness.

Just like that day twelve years ago she felt it again, hitting her hard, taking her breath for just an instant before she reminded herself that he was a two-timing, no-good piece of work that she wanted nothing to do with.

Yes, he'd tried to make amends. There were

times she might even still consider him a friend. But she couldn't let herself get pulled in by his looks and charm. Not again.

She was just in a vulnerable state because she was tired, hungry and…tired.

"Holly," he started.

She shook her head. The room spun a little and felt a need to put some distance between them. She took a step back.

"What are you doing here?" she heard herself ask him. It was a silly question. His family lived here. And it wasn't the first time he'd come home. Nor the first time she'd seen him in the past eleven years.

It's just that he never came here, not to the café.

"I'm sorry, I know it's a shock. I just need a few minutes of your time."

"Why?"

He had moved closer and was suddenly in front of her, too real, smelling too good. She nearly groaned at her own weakness for this man.

All because years ago he'd given her six-year-old self a kitten. He told her she needed that kitten more than he did because she needed to smile more. And she had. She'd needed both the kitten and his friendship.

"Spit it out, Colt." He remained silent, and she started to walk away.

"Not here," he finally told her.

He wasn't the boy she'd met all those years ago. He wasn't even the man she'd met up with at college. The man in front of her had laugh lines at the corners of his eyes and he'd broadened across the chest and shoulders. He had a small scar on his forehead, where he'd been kicked by the bull that had taken him down.

"Couldn't you have just sent an email?" she asked.

"Afraid not." He lowered his voice. "Not this time."

"Colt, could you head on down the road," Martin Finley said as he stuck his fingers in Chet Duncan's ice water. "I've got three burned fingers and coffee in my fries. You're like yesterday's bad news."

"Not until I get some business taken care of." Colt continued to stare at her and Holly felt her self-control unraveling. She'd had a horrible morning and he was making this a terrible afternoon so far.

Why oh why did he have to be the prettiest man she'd ever laid eyes on? His dark lashes and quicksilver eyes just about did a girl in.

"Does your dad know you're home?" some-one in the diner asked Colt.

"I didn't come home to see Jack." Colt low-ered his voice, making it obvious the con-versation was between the two of them. He caught her gaze and held it. "I came to see Holly."

She nodded and glanced around, looking for the waitress still on duty. "Stacy, could you take over for me?"

"Sure thing, boss." Stacy was already on it. She had a mop, a towel and a look that said she'd handle things. And that included Colt, if need be.

"We need privacy for this conversation," he told her, his voice reminding her of coffee on a cold winter morning. Coffee, strong and with the right amount of sugar and cream.

"Fine," she told him. "We can talk in the back dining area."

She led the way to the back room, typically used for overflow or private parties and he followed at a slower pace. She had a minute to breathe, to regain control.

He closed the door behind them and she turned to face him.

"Have you decided to call in the loan, or maybe sell your percentage of the café? I know you, and whatever brought you here it isn't going to make my life any easier, is it?"

Her life was hard enough as it was. The café was doing well but her mother's health was failing. Holly hadn't had a good night's sleep in what felt like years. The last thing she needed was Colt showing up, disturbing the tenuous balance of her life.

"Really, that's what you think of me?" His eyes narrowed, he looked hurt. "Holly, I haven't asked for a payment. I haven't given you advice. I don't come in and give my opinions. I think I'm the model silent partner."

"You are and I'm sorry. But there's a reason you're here and that's the only one I could think of. Is your dad okay?"

"Jack's fine. I'm not here about Jack. I'm here because we need to have a conversation."

That was the last thing she thought they needed to do. As strong as she thought she might be, he had a way of chipping at her defenses. He would make her feel pretty, feel special and then feel broken. He'd done it before. She had a lot of reasons to protect her heart from Colt West.

He motioned her toward a table, even pulled out a chair for her.

She took the seat and he sat across from

her, tossing his hat on the table and running both hands through his hair like he meant to pull it out.

"Get it over with, please. I can't take much more of this. Are you sick? Did that bull hurt you worse than everyone said?"

He looked up, his head still resting in hands that were buried in his hair. He grimaced as he leaned back. "I'm not sick. I would tell you not to worry but I doubt worry is the first thing you feel for me."

"I would be upset if something happened to you," she admitted, her voice faltering.

"This isn't about the accident. I'm healing up fine. I'll hopefully be back to work at the end of May."

"But until then, you're here to make my life difficult?"

"No, I'm not." He leaned back in his chair and studied her face. "You're still beautiful."

Of course he would go there. That was his way of dealing with life. He charmed. He complimented.

Holly, you'll always be my best friend. He'd told her that when she turned nine and he was ten. He'd given her a wilted bouquet of wild-flowers as he made the promise.

"Don't. I don't want your compliments and

I don't want you trying to take me down rabbit trails. You're obviously here on business. So why don't we cut to the chase?"

He didn't smile. "Of course, right to the point. I'm not here about the café."

Raising her arm, she made a show of checking the time on her watch. "I do have a business to run. *Our* business. Remember, I send you a check each month."

He shoved himself up from the table and limped to the window. His hand rubbed the back of his neck.

"Holly, it's about Dixie. That's why I'm here."

Dixie.

He wasn't here about the café or about them. He was here to tell her something concerning Dixie.

Their daughter.

Chapter Two

Holly's world tilted and everything started to dim. She became aware of Colt at her side telling her to breathe as he shoved her head down between her knees. She breathed because it seemed necessary, but then she sat back up, pushing his hand away.

"Dixie?" she whispered, afraid to say the word out loud. "Is she hurt? Or sick?" she asked. "What's happened."

He backed away from her. "I think it's time to clear the restaurant."

"Clear the restaurant? Why?"

"Give me a minute to deal with your customers."

She nodded, agreeing. "Have Stacy send everyone home for the day. Tell them there's a family emergency."

He paused at the door. "I'll take care of it. And I'll have her bring you a glass of water."

A glass of water was the last thing she wanted. She wanted answers. She needed to know that Dixie was okay. No, she hadn't raised her daughter, but that hadn't diminished her love for the tiny baby she'd held, then handed over to another woman to raise. She'd always loved her daughter, and if something had happened to her, surely she'd sense it. Wouldn't she?

From the main dining room she heard Isaac, not Colt, telling customers they were going to have to leave due to a family emergency. A few of her customers questioned him. Chet Duncan flat-out asked him what Colt had done to Holly. Isaac assured them Holly would be fine, but the café would be closed until further notice.

Until further notice? That's not what she'd told Colt. She started toward the main dining room but then Colt returned, stopping her. He wasn't alone. Standing next to him was a girl. A girl of eleven who looked like the perfect combination of the two of them.

It was hard to breathe, hard to think. She wanted to move but her feet seemed to be glued to the floor. Her vision swam as tears filled her eyes.

"Colt, what have you done? Because this isn't like bringing me a kitten. You can't just take a child."

"I've done this all wrong," Colt said as if surprised that he could ever be wrong. But what did she expect from Colt?

She expected him to break her heart, to shatter the life she was building for herself. That's what she expected because that's all he'd ever done.

No, that wasn't true. Once upon a time he'd been her best friend, always doing little things to make her smile or laugh.

She blinked away the tears.

"Dixie." Her voice broke as she took a step forward. "Are you okay?"

Her daughter was here, just feet away from her, holding herself ramrod stiff. Holly wanted to pull her close. She wanted to reassure herself that the child was real and whole and unharmed.

"I, uh…" The girl looked from Colt to Holly, her silver-gray eyes—Colt's eyes—suddenly unsure. "I'm fine."

Holly cataloged the rest of the girl's features. Her nose, her mouth, her honey-brown hair. A little bit of her was Holly. The mouth. The wave in her hair. The freckles on her nose.

For eleven years she'd mourned the loss of this child. For eleven birthdays she'd cherished photos sent to keep her updated on her daughter's life.

"You're here." Holly shook her head and pinned Colt with a look. "She shouldn't be here. Colt, why is she here?"

Holly closed the distance between them. Dixie stood straight, as if barely holding herself together. Silver-gray eyes shimmered with unshed tears, but the girl, just a child really, didn't let them fall. Without asking, Holly wrapped her arms around her daughter and held her, keeping her close until that ramrod stiffness dissolved. Because this was where the two of them might be the most alike. Holly knew all about holding it together, staying strong, not letting people see her weaknesses.

Captured in Holly's embrace, the child fell apart, her sobs coming in heavy waves.

Colt walked away, taking a seat at a table some twenty feet from them.

Holly held her daughter until the tears started to subside.

"I'm not sure what's going on," Holly murmured against her daughter's head. "But I'm glad to have this chance to meet you."

"Me, too," Dixie sniffled against her shoulder. "I kind of can't breathe."

Holly released her daughter. Dixie shuddered a little, then wiped her eyes with her hands. Holly grabbed a few napkins from a dispenser on a nearby table.

"Let's sit down and figure this all out."

She walked Dixie to the table where Colt had taken a seat. He looked more unsure than she'd ever seen him, except once. The day Dixie had been born. The day they hugged their baby girl, prayed for her and turned her over to Becky Stafford.

She looked at Colt. "Explain," she said. "Because this is not the birthday gift I expected today."

He smacked his forehead. "I forgot your birthday. I knew there had to be a reason you're so upset with me."

He winked at their daughter. Dixie giggled just a little. Enough to lighten the ache in Holly's chest.

Holly gave him a warning look. "I need to know what is going on."

"My mom had a heart attack," Dixie said softly, her voice breaking as she answered.

"I'm so sorry," Holly said, wanting to gather the girl up in her arms again and hold her. Dixie leaned back a little, as if knowing Holly's thoughts. Holly shifted her attention back to Colt.

"What do you say we get Dixie settled and we can talk later?" he said with a meaningful look in Dixie's direction.

"Yes, later, of course." Holly pushed her seat back but she didn't stand. She had so many questions and it seemed as if he was purposely avoiding answering them. "Where are you staying?"

He rubbed a hand across his stubbly cheek and had the good sense to turn a bit red in the face. "A few years back I bought the old Miller place. It was a good investment and I thought maybe someday I might come back to Hope. That's where I've stayed the couple of times I've been to town."

"A mile from my house. You own a home a mile from mine?"

"This is getting awkward," Dixie said in a dry tone. "Do I get a say in where I'm staying?"

They looked at each other, she and Colt. Did Dixie get a say? Holly had no idea because she didn't know what was going on.

"I don't know. Colt, does she get a say?"

Colt pushed himself to his feet and leaned heavily on the cane. "Yes, you get a say."

"I've been with you for a week. I'd like to know my mom a little better. After all, that's why I'm here, isn't it?" Dixie followed Colt's lead and stood.

She wanted to stay with her mom? Holly sat there for a few seconds, then it hit her. She was the mom Dixie spoke of. She was the person Dixie wanted to stay with.

"Is that okay?" Dixie asked, suddenly acting her age and showing her uncertainty with the situation and with them.

"I…" Holly hesitated, thinking about her mother. "Yes, of course."

Dixie's attention suddenly switched to Colt. He looked at both of them, then nodded.

"Does that mean we can go?" Dixie asked.

"I have a few things to take care of," Holly told her. "But yes, we can go."

Holly left them in the dining room, hurrying to the kitchen. She needed a minute to breathe, to cry, to compose herself.

"You okay, boss?" Jim, her fry cook, stopped wiping down the counters and tossed the rag in the sink. "Anything I can do?"

"I'll be fine, but thank you." She turned to the woman who waited tables but managed any number of problems for Holly. "Stacy, could you make sure everything is taken care of? Just close up and go home for the evening. I'm not sure if we'll open tomorrow. I'll let you both know."

The two of them waited for more of an explanation. Holly closed her eyes and pinched the bridge of her nose to stop the tears from falling. Her eyes opened as arms went around her, pulling her in for a quick hug. A tear trickled down her cheek. A hugger who rarely included Holly in her affectionate embraces, Stacy released her but the caring in her hazel eyes struck a chord in Holly. She'd always been on the outside of most friend groups.

She was no longer the shy little girl who kept to herself. She had friends now.

"Leave it to me," Stacy said. "And if you want, I can open for breakfast and lunch tomorrow. Just say the word."

Holly bit down on her bottom lip and looked from the woman who had been her best help to the cook who could do his job blindfolded.

"Holly, I've worked for you for three years. I can do this. And a day off would be good for you. Sleep in. Take care of whatever is going on, and trust me." Stacy's gaze shifted to Jim. "We've got this, right, Jim?"

He nodded but remained silent. She knew her employees counted on their weekly salary. A day closed meant a day's pay gone.

"I do trust you." She looked around the kitchen, sparkling clean and ready for the following day. This café had been her dream for years. She'd come home to work for Mattie, and when Mattie decided to retire, Holly had prayed for a way to buy the place.

Colt had shown up, lurking around town, watching his dad from a distance but still too angry to approach him. But he'd had the nerve to approach Holly. She remembered how it had felt to see him standing at the edge of the lake, waiting for her to arrive. He'd smiled, as if they were still best friends. She'd been wrapped up in a past that felt like a coat of too many colors. Anger, hurt, bittersweet emotions of childhood, love and sadness, all swirling around deep inside her.

They'd managed to talk without her killing him and she'd told him about Mattie's Café. And now, here they were, business partners, parents, still barely able to manage the past that would always be between them.

"We've got this." Stacy drew her back to

the present with words of assurance. "And it seems you have bigger fish to fry. If you need anything, Holly, I'm here."

"Thank you." She glanced toward the door, and through the window she could see the dining room where her daughter stood at Colt's side.

"You need to take the weekend off, Holly."

"Okay, you're right." Holly exhaled. "Call in Evelyn if you need help tomorrow."

"Got it. Now go home." Stacy took her by the shoulders and steered her toward the door. "I'll take care of the café. You take care of yourself."

Holly returned to the dining room. Dixie and Colt had moved to the front door. Isaac had left. There was an awkward moment that settled over them as they stood there together.

"Let's go to your place," Colt suggested as he reached to push the door open.

"Of course." They had to start somewhere. "My place it is."

The place where her mother resided. Colt knew her mother; he knew the struggles of Holly's childhood. True, Opal wasn't the same person she'd been twenty years ago. That didn't make it any easier to think about taking a child into her home. It really only meant the surfacing of old memories and old wounds.

Dixie sighed. "The two of you have to stop acting so unsure. You're the adults, and all of this uncertainty makes me feel insecure."

Colt laughed a little. "We've got this, Dixie."

"Do you? I'm not so sure. You left my allergy medicine at Daisy's. You forgot that I'm eleven and I have to go to school. There's a lot of responsibility when you have a kid," Dixie reminded Colt.

"There is definitely a lot of responsibility when you have a child," Holly said with what she hoped sounded like a measure of confidence. Except she didn't know if she had a child, not really. She only knew that Dixie was here with Colt, Becky Stafford had passed away, and at home she had a mother who was slowly slipping away from reality.

Her gaze connected with Colt's and she felt anything but confident. They had a lot to say to each other and none of it easy. They had a past. They had a daughter. And now it appeared they wouldn't be walking out of each other's lives anytime soon.

Colt followed Holly up the driveway to the gingerbread-trim farmhouse that had been in her family for several generations. It had seen better times. The siding had faded, the flower gardens were overgrown with weeds, and the fences sagged.

He drove past the house and parked his truck and trailer near the barn. As he got out of the truck his horse whinnied, thinking he was finally home.

"Not quite," Colt told the animal.

He headed toward the front yard, his left leg protesting the fast walk that narrowed the distance between himself and Holly. She was out of her car, Dixie at her side. He paused mid-stride because an incredible sense of "this is how it should have been" overcame him. As he stood there looking at the woman he had quietly loved, the woman he'd hurt more than any other, and the daughter they'd given up for adoption, he realized what he'd missed out on.

For a long minute he got caught up, thinking of the past, the present and the realization that a man couldn't go back in time and right the wrongs he'd created. He couldn't undo the fact that he'd never been faithful to a woman, including the one who had become the mother of his child.

Guilt pounded against him, relentless and

unforgiving like the winds of a hurricane hitting the shore.

Standing in front of him was a second chance to do things the right way. But he had a strong feeling Holly probably wasn't in a forgiving mood.

"Are you going to wait out here?" Dixie called out. She moved closer to Holly's side trying to act confident, but he knew better.

"We should go in," Holly said with a voice that trembled. Her teeth worried her bottom lip as she glanced toward the house. "I should warn you both that my mother, Opal, isn't well."

Her words didn't surprise him. Opal had never been well. Holly's mother had struggled with mental illness all her life. She'd self-medicated with drugs and alcohol. After Holly's father had passed away, her mother had worked hard and tried her best to give Holly some stability.

"What's wrong with her?" Dixie asked. "Is it her heart?"

Holly shook her head. "No, it isn't. She struggles with depression but now she has some memory loss and balance issues. It makes life a challenge."

If the dark circles under Holly's eyes or the

weight loss were any indication, he would guess that Opal had real struggles and Holly was doing her best to keep things going.

They walked up to the front door. A faded Christmas wreath hung from a hook; the cedar boughs had turned brown and pine cones hung loosely as if the glue had given up. Holly looked at that wreath and for a brief second her eyes closed.

"I obviously need to spend a day or two on the house," she said, then smiled down at Dixie. "I can cook, but I've never been the best with a dustrag."

"I'm good at dusting," Dixie offered. "And I do dishes."

"Do you?" Holly's smile brightened her face. "We might make a pretty good team. If…"

Holly looked at him, her eyes narrowing. He knew what she was thinking, that she didn't know if Dixie would be staying. Unfortunately, he didn't know their future, either.

Holly pushed the front door open just as the smoke detector began to beep. The shrill sound echoed through the house, accompanied by the smell of smoke.

"Oh no." Holly hurried through the house to the kitchen.

Dixie and Colt followed close behind. He remembered the house well from his childhood visits. A front living room, a hall that led past a tiny parlor to the kitchen, the dining room in the back, and bedrooms upstairs. At some point a porch had been converted into a sitting room with windows that faced the fields.

They found Holly and Opal in the kitchen. Opal held her hand under running water and in the opposite side of the sink a pan sizzled. Boiled eggs littered the hardwood floor.

"Mom, what were you doing?" Holly rummaged in the cabinet and pulled out a jar. "Remember the signs. They tell you what to eat and they tell you…" Holly shook her head. "Of course you don't remember."

"I tried to remember," Opal said, smiling at them. "We have company. My goodness, is that Holly? It's been so long since I've seen her."

"Mom, I'm Holly."

Opal seemed confused by that. "You're Holly. Of course you are. Is my mother visiting today?"

"No." Holly dabbed salve on her mother's hand. "This will help the burn."

"It smells like my tea." Opal raised her hand. "Dandelions?"

"Lavender."

"I see. I really hurt myself."

"Yes, you did." Holly held her mother's hand, the skin red from the heat of the burn. "Oh, Mom, what are we going to do?"

"It's your birthday," Opal whispered. "I wanted to make deviled eggs for your birthday. I wanted to make kites. The strawberry with strawberry icing."

"Cake," Holly corrected.

She ignored the correction and looked around. "I have to clean this mess."

"No, go sit in your room and I'll clean up. Remember Colt?" Holly asked her mother as she moved her in the direction of the sitting room.

"He's a no-good…"

Dixie laughed. Fortunately Opal didn't finish her description of his personal faults. He obviously had plenty. He guessed it would be wasted breath to tell them he was doing his best, working on being a better man.

As he watched, Dixie introduced herself to Opal and the two moved over to the sitting room, discussing kittens and cake as they went. His gaze slid to the woman standing next to him. She looked like she needed a shoulder to lean on. Probably any shoulder but his.

Her expression shuttered as she grabbed a broom from the corner of the kitchen.

"Let me help you clean this up," he offered.

"I've got it." She swept, deposited broken pieces of egg in the trash and then returned for paper towels. Ignoring him, she dropped to her knees and began to clean the floor.

"Holly, please let me help." Colt made the uncomfortable journey to kneel next to her. He took the paper towels from her clenched hand and wiped down the floor, picking up pieces that hadn't been swept up. She remained next to him, silently watching as he cleaned up the rest of the mess.

"If you had a dog, this would be much easier." He reached for the counter with his free hand and pulled himself to his feet, feeling a sharp jab of pain in his leg.

"You should have let me do it." She took the hand he offered and he pulled her to standing. He didn't let go of her go, instead lacing his fingers through hers. She studied their intertwined hands.

Without asking, he wrapped his free arm around her and pulled her close, holding her in his arms for a moment until the tension eased and she took a deep breath. Her head rested on his shoulder and he guessed she forgot that he was the last man she should ever trust.

Never in his life had he wanted, more than anything, to be the man she could trust. He wanted to be someone she could count on.

"I'm fine," she said as she slipped from his embrace. She took the paper towels and headed for the trash can. "Colt, I can't take this. You have to tell me what is going on."

"I know. Let me check on your mom and Dixie first, then we'll step outside and talk."

With a quick nod, she went out the back door. He watched as she stood at the edge of the patio, then she headed toward his trailer. He entered the sitting room, stopping for a moment to watch as Dixie tried to explain who she was to Opal.

"She doesn't know who I am?" Dixie asked. "Does she have Alzheimer's? She isn't that old."

He sat down on a footstool and smiled at Opal. He'd always liked Holly's mother. She was different. That's what most people in Hope said about Opal. She'd had Holly late in life, returning to town with her young daughter to live with her elderly mother. It had been the three of them against the world. Millie, Holly's aging grandmother, Opal, a woman who had struggled with addiction for most of her life, and Holly. It had never been a normal home, not in the way most people thought of.

"I don't think it's Alzheimer's," he answered. "Opal has struggled with a lot of things in her life. Opal, do you know that Dixie is your granddaughter? She's Holly's little baby."

Opal smiled and reached for Dixie's hand. The two sat next to each other, looking more alike than he would have guessed. They had the same dimples, the same quirky smile.

"I know who she is, Colt." Opal sighed. "I'm so glad she's here. I'm moving and I wouldn't want Holly to be alone."

"Moving?" Colt hesitated, wondering if Opal might be slipping into the past again.

"I've talked to your brother and I think I need to go to Lakeside Manor. I'd like for you to help Holly understand. I can't…" She shook her head. "I don't know the words, Colt."

"I'll talk to her," he said.

"She won't listen. She's stubborn, like her father. He was a banker, you know."

"Was he?" He wondered if Holly knew.

"I have to plant flowers." Opal stood. "Will you help me plant flowers, Holly?"

"I'm Dixie." Dixie rose, her face pale as she looked from her grandmother to Colt.

"Yes, I know. But we have to plant the flowers as a surprise for my mother." Opal slid her feet into slippers.

"Can you go outside with her?" Colt asked his daughter.

"I think so." Dixie bit down on her bottom lip, much like Holly did.

"If you need anything, just holler for me."

She nodded and allowed Opal to lead her from the room. Colt watched them go, then headed for the back door—and Holly. It seemed they had more to talk about than just custody of Dixie.

His empty, selfish life was now about more than the next rodeo. It was about being a better version of himself. For Dixie and for Holly, because they both were going to need him.

Chapter Three

Holly pretended not to notice Colt heading her way. She'd unlatched the back of his trailer and moved inside to back his horse out. The animal greeted her with a soft whinny, turning to rub his big autumn-red head against her shoulder.

"You want out of here, don't you? Even if it's for a few minutes." She moved a panel and the horse stomped, impatient to be free from the enclosure.

"I think horse theft is still a crime in the great state of Oklahoma." Colt's voice echoed inside the trailer.

"Consider it animal rescue and not theft," she returned. The lighter mood settled easily around her heart. She'd needed a few minutes to breathe through the last hour.

It took a person more than a minute to adjust to the appearance of a daughter she'd
never thought to see again. In all of her hopes
and prayers she'd never thought of Dixie losing the woman who had been her mother.
Her greatest hope had been that at eighteen,
Becky would allow them to meet.

But Becky had always been Dixie's mother,
even in those dreams.

"Are you okay?" His soft voice ricocheted
off the trailer walls.

"Yeah, I'm better." She led his horse from
the trailer, the metal-shod hooves beating a
rhythm on its floor. The animal tugged at the
lead rope. She spoke gently and he flicked an
ear to listen.

"You like her, Bounty?" Colt took the lead
rope from his horse and the animal nodded
his head. "Is that right? Is she the woman
you've prayed for?"

He made a motion and the horse knelt with
one front leg stretched forward and his head
dropped low.

Holly couldn't help but laugh. "That's
cheesy."

"But is it effective cheesiness?" he asked.
"We can do more."

"I'm sure you can." Her expression softened. "I've missed you. I don't even like admitting that, but it's true."

"I know." He patted his horse's neck and slipped him a sugar cube from his pocket. He raised his gaze to meet hers. "I know that missing me is the last thing you would want to do."

"With good reason. You really hurt me, Colt."

"I know and I'm sorry."

She just looked at him.

"Can I turn him out in the corral for a few minutes?"

"Sure, go ahead. I can't guarantee the quality of the fences, though."

"He won't go anywhere."

She walked with him as he led the horse to a gate that still latched, but the hinges were rusted and one set had come loose. He eased the gate open and turned the horse into the small area.

"I have so much work I need to catch up on." She glanced around, sighing because sometimes it was just too much. The fences, the house, the yard. Opal.

She spotted her at the front of the house with Dixie. They were pulling weeds and talking. Her mother laughed and Dixie smiled. What would it have been like, to raise Dixie here?

"Don't look back," Colt warned. "It doesn't do any good. We have to remember why we made the decision we made."

"There were plenty of reasons," she admitted. "I was too young and I knew you wouldn't be the man I needed you to be."

"I'd already proven that."

"Yes." Her heart ached as she said the word, remembering how it had felt to see him in the arms of another woman. She'd just learned she was pregnant and had been eager to tell him. She blinked away the memory, not wanting to evoke those feelings and emotions today. Today was about Dixie. She was the present, not the past.

"I'm sorry," he said.

"I know. But what about now? What about Dixie?"

He limped to the trailer door. "Let me get the paperwork. I want everything on the table because we have decisions to make."

"Okay." Her heart hammered at the seriousness of his tone.

He stepped up into the trailer and motioned her inside. She followed, although her instincts told her to go in the other direction.

"I'm not sure we should be in here. Opal and Dixie might need us." She stopped talking and turned to take in the opulence of the trailer. "This is your horse trailer? This is ridiculous."

He pulled a file from a cabinet and glanced around. "Yeah, it's more of a home than anything else I own."

"What else do you own, other than the old Miller place?"

"That's about it." He glanced at the file.

"Colt?" She tossed him a look.

He sighed. "A condo in Florida and some land in Texas. The condo is an investment. The land in Texas..." He shrugged. "A dream."

"Dreams are good." They walked back out and headed for the patio. "Are you okay?"

"Of course, why?"

"I thought you would have recovered from your injuries by now. It's been a couple of months, hasn't it?"

"It's been slow going, slower than I expected."

"But you'll go back to work. And then what? What about Dixie?"

"That's what we have to talk about."

They reached the concrete patio at the back

of the house and took seats at the patio table. He slid the folder across the table.

"You can read it but it's probably easier if I just tell you. But first, before we have that discussion, I need to tell you what Opal told me."

"Opal? What could she possibly tell you that is more important than this?" Holly opened the file to peruse the legal documents inside.

"Your mom told me she's talked to Carson about being admitted to Lakeside Manor."

She shook her head at the suggestion. "No. I'm not putting her in a nursing home."

"Holly, I'm only telling you what she told me. I don't have any advice on the subject. She wanted you to know. I think this is a decision she wants to make while she's able."

"She isn't able. There are days she thinks I'm her mother. There are days she thinks my father, the illustrious banker, has called to tell her he's coming back to her. He never married her. He didn't want us. I feel like I'm an instant replay of her life."

Never really wanted.

Colt pulled back as if she'd physically slapped him. She didn't care. His hurt feelings were nothing compared to the maelstrom of emotions this day had wrought.

"I think you have to consider her feelings," he chimed in. She knew she had to consider her mother's feelings.

"I don't need you to tell me how to make decisions."

"I know. But Holly, you can't always be with her…"

"Then I'll hire someone," she snapped at him.

"You're wearing yourself out," he continued. He wasn't making brownie points with observations like that one. She knew very well how she looked and how she felt.

"I don't want to have this discussion on top of the conversation about Dixie. Let's refocus on our daughter."

"Gotcha, one tough subject at a time." Colt leaned back in the chair.

She avoided looking his direction, because if she looked at him, if she saw the sympathy in his silver-gray eyes, she'd fall apart. He'd always been her weakness.

"This situation is complicated," Colt started. "My sister Daisy spent quite a bit of her teen years with Becky. Daisy settled in Tulsa after her divorce so she, Dixie and Becky were kind of a family unit."

Daisy, Holly's childhood friend, had been

close to Dixie, closer than Holly herself. The first stirrings of jealousy swirled through her belly.

"Okay," she prodded, needing more.

"Becky knew she had congestive heart failure and she prepared a will. She left everything in trust for Dixie, with Daisy as administrator. She also wanted for us to have time to get to know Dixie." He paused, shifting his hat to block the late-afternoon sun.

"Colt, what does that mean?"

"Custody is Dixie's decision. She will be with us until the end of May. That gives her two months to make a decision. She can choose to stay with us or she can go back to Tulsa—and Daisy."

"She's only eleven. How can she make a decision about what is best for her?"

"Holly, I'm sorry."

"No." She raised a hand to stop him from saying more. "I don't know how to process all of this. I thought…" She let out a jagged breath that hurt.

"Becky left a letter for us, asking us to do our very best for our daughter. She didn't leave it entirely up to Dixie. She asked us to include Dixie in any decision that is made but she asked us to be aware that Dixie and

Daisy have a bond. Daisy will never keep her from us."

Holly brushed away the tears that slid down her cheeks.

"What else?" Holly asked, because she was sure there had to be more.

"We have to be able to share custody in a way that won't hurt our daughter."

"How is that possible when you don't even live here? Would I have her for a week here and you take her for a week at the beach or in Texas, or on the road with you?"

Calm. She needed to be calm. Even she could hear her voice rising as she thought about the heartache for Dixie, for Daisy and for herself and Colt. She understood that Becky had been trying to make the best decision for Dixie, but Holly couldn't believe this was best.

"I'm not leaving," Colt surprised her by saying. "I'm going to be here, helping Dixie to get settled. I've given this a lot of thought."

"Because you had more than one day to adjust."

His cheeks turned red at her accusation. "Yes, I did have more time. During that time I've thought about us, and what we can do to make things work out for our daughter."

His words sank in, and she laughed because surely he couldn't be proposing that they…no, this wasn't a proposal. "Please don't tell me you think we should get married?"

He cleared his throat. "Well, yes, actually I do think we should get married."

"At nineteen I would have given anything to be your wife." Her heart broke a little as she spoke. "I loved you. Maybe I still do love you a little. Unfortunately you broke my heart. I'm not going to be my mother. She thought a man loved her, then she found out he was married to someone else. I'm not going to do this, Colt. I won't drag Dixie into a relationship that isn't built on trust. We can't get married just to make a family for our daughter."

"I think it's the best reason to get married."

"No, it isn't." She stood, stacking the papers so she could insert them back in the file. "I'd like to keep this and look over it."

"Be my guest. That's your copy."

He pushed himself to his feet and towered over her from the other side of the table. That made her mad. She wasn't a small woman. She'd always been above average height. And she didn't cower before men. But he had a way of shaking her up, making her feel things she didn't want to feel.

Right at that moment she felt regret because once, a long time ago, she'd wanted to marry him. She'd thought he would be the one to make her life into a fairy tale. She'd wanted him to ride in and fix everything for her.

"If it makes a difference, I'm sorry. I've been sorry every day for almost twelve years. If I could take back what I did to you…" Colt shrugged.

"I've forgiven you, Colt. I should also thank you for teaching me something about myself. I'm strong. Much stronger than I ever thought. What I learned is that I don't need you to fix my life. I found that I needed to be happy with myself, with my life, and it was wrong to think I needed another person to bring me happiness."

"Well—" he grinned, but it was with a hint of sadness "—I'm glad I could be of service."

"Colt, we have to find a way to do this without resorting to extremes. We can be the parents Dixie needs. We can work together to make her feel safe and loved."

"I agree," he said as he rounded the table to stand close to her. "But I'm not giving up on us."

"There is no us."

He leaned over and kissed her cheek. "I don't want to argue with you, darlin', but I've been praying on something and I'm not quite ready to give up."

Her heart stuttered at his words but she pulled away, willing herself to remember her strength. "I'm glad you're praying."

He winked. "I know that takes you by surprise. God and I have been working on building a new relationship. So I'm going to head on over to my place and leave Dixie here with you. But you've been warned, Holly, and I don't plan on giving up too easy."

"Warned about what?" Opal asked as she came around the corner of the house. "Is there a tornado?"

"No, Mom, it's just Colt being silly."

"Well, I made egg salad for supper. Colt, would you like to stay?" Opal looked down at her dirty hands. "I think I've been in the mud. I need to go wash up."

"Mom, we'll go inside in a minute. Colt is leaving." Holly felt her whole world shift as her gaze collided with his. She looked away before he could make her regret. "Dixie, if you're okay with staying here, we'll get your room ready."

Dixie nodded but didn't look settled on

the fact. She looked to Colt. "Will you be here Sunday? Remember, you said we'd go to church together. And I can meet my grandpa, Jack?"

"That's the plan. But if Holly doesn't mind, I'll also come by tomorrow. Maybe we can throw some burgers on the grill."

His flirty grin had returned.

"That would be fine."

"Dixie, give me a hug goodbye. And if you need me, I'm just down the road."

Holly watched their farewells, then she herded her mother and Dixie back into the house. From the kitchen window she watched as Colt led his horse back to the trailer. She knew that Colt was the last thing she needed in her life.

But it seemed he was in her life anyway. For better or for worse.

Colt would have liked to say he drove off without looking back. That wouldn't have been the truth, and he'd been working hard on being a more honest person. A better man. That had been his goal for the past year, since God had shaken him up one night with a nightmare that had been like a trip down memory lane. He had hurt a lot of people in his life.

This time as he drove away from Holly's he couldn't help but think about the two people he was leaving behind. But not leaving. He'd be here tomorrow and the next day. He'd be in their lives every day if they'd let him. Both of them had choices. Dixie would choose if she wanted to live with Daisy or them. Holly would choose if she wanted to give him another chance.

He hit his blinker and turned right, onto a paved drive that led to a ranch-style home built in the 1970s. He liked the house, with its big windows, large rooms, views of the countryside and the fences made of treated lumber. The barn was dark brown metal with a big corral. He hadn't spent more than a few days here since he'd bought the place. As far as he knew, few people were aware that he was the owner.

Including his father, Jack West, the owner of the now famous Mercy Ranch. A ranch for wounded military veterans trying to rebuild their lives. A ranch for people like the man Jack West had been when he came home from Vietnam. A broken man who'd married a younger woman, a nurse who had helped care for him.

He couldn't deny that his gut was tied in knots just thinking about a reunion with his father. He'd almost rather get trampled by another bull.

Once upon a time, Jack had been meaner than old Snake Bite, the bull that Colt had tangled with recently. These days Jack was twenty years older and a lot more mellow. He'd given up booze and fighting, had sought out help, and had gotten right with God.

Colt was very glad all three had happened for his dad.

He pulled his trailer up to the metal barn, and as he got out, he noticed he had company.

Isaac got out of his truck, and from the passenger seat, their older brother, Carson, exited and headed his way. That was a surprise. He might have expected Isaac to follow him to the house but he kind of thought Carson, a doctor, would be at home with his wife and children.

"So it is true that you own this place?" Isaac asked with a grin as he surveyed the property. "Nice place. I didn't expect to see you here, though."

"Where'd you expect to see me?" Colt

asked as he headed for the back of his trailer. "Hi to you, too, Carson."

"Little brother, good to see you again."

"Right." Colt unlatched the back of the gate. "How's Kylie? Is she still glad that I sent you back here to propose?"

"I reckon she is." Carson, always the serious one, grinned. Love did that to a man.

"I thought you would stick pretty close to Holly's, what with your daughter here and all." Isaac interrupted them with all the finesse of the proverbial bull rampaging through a china shop.

Isaac was nothing if not charming. It was one of the things he and his half brother had in common.

"I thought it best to give the two of them a night together. I've had Dixie for a few days. She's probably sick of me."

"You're the familiar face now," Carson interjected. Colt didn't remember asking his opinion.

"Yeah, well, I can't say that I'm the best one to help her adjust to her new life, the one where she doesn't have a mother."

They all got quiet.

Isaac pulled a wrapped toothpick from his pocket and tore the cellophane away. The trash went in his pocket; the toothpick went between his teeth. He didn't say anything but he shot a glance in Carson's direction, obviously deciding the older of the three had more to say about the situation.

"Go ahead and tell me what I've done wrong. I'm sure you've got a long list." Colt tensed as he waited. He and Carson locked gazes the way a couple of old bulls would lock horns.

They didn't have a reason to be at odds. It had just happened somewhere along the way. Maybe because they'd gone different directions with their lives. Colt enjoyed rodeo more than he enjoyed settling down. Carson had always needed a neat and orderly life.

Isaac had been here in Hope, with Jack, since Colt and Carson's mom hauled them out of town. He'd adjusted, and somehow had done the impossible: he'd been the catalyst for Jack getting sober.

Colt's life had always been messy. And it got under his skin that Isaac was standing there looking like the family man and favorite son.

Carson finally cleared his throat and shrugged.

"I can't say a thing. It isn't like I always

make the right decisions. Remember, you showed up in Chicago to let me know that I was messing up." Carson shrugged. "We've all got our stuff to figure out. We just don't want Dixie to have more to deal with than she can handle."

Colt pulled off his hat and ran a hand through his too-long hair. "I know. I mean, look at us. We aren't exactly poster children for stable and functional."

"Speak for yourself," Isaac quipped as he pointed to himself. "Married with a beautiful wife, daughter and another one on the way."

"So what do I do?" Colt asked, knowing full well that he wouldn't like their answers.

"I think you need to stay close. Let Dixie know that you're here for her. And it might be good for Holly to know that you're here to help her out," Carson replied in his typical matter-of-fact tone.

Colt shoved his hat back on his head. "Holly doesn't need me or want me to be there for her."

"You think women tell you when they need help with something?" Isaac laughed and slapped Colt on the back. "You don't know as much about women as you let on."

"They like me. I like them. What more do I need to know?"

Isaac arched a brow. "That statement proves how little you know. Let me explain in the simplest terms so you can understand."

Colt glared. Isaac just smiled and continued. "A woman isn't always going to tell you when she needs help. She'll give you clues. But when you ask her why she's mad or if she needs something, she's going to say there's nothing wrong. But then she'll stomp past you with a ladder, and you'll understand that there is definitely something she wanted from you and it probably has nothing to do with the football game you're watching."

"Sounds as if you're speaking from experience," Colt said as he went to lead his horse from the trailer. He stepped inside to untie the gelding and back him out.

"It's something you'll learn in time. If you stick around, that is." Isaac leaned against the side of the trailer. "Nice animal."

Colt led the horse out, holding the lead rope as the animal shook like a dog, sending dust flying. "He's tired of that trailer."

"Can't say that I blame him," Carson spoke up, his expression more than a little amused. Probably due to Isaac's anecdote about women.

"I plan on sticking around. If Holly wants me to." Colt led his horse in the direction of the corral. Bounty trotted next to him, eager for the water trough and green grass. "I'm not exactly sure she wants me in her life."

"She probably needs convincing that you're in this with her."

"I asked her to marry me. How much more could I be in this?"

Carson laughed at that. Isaac groaned.

"How did that go over?" Carson asked after another round of laughter, this time with Isaac joining in.

"Glad you all are so amused."

"You can't complain if we laugh." Isaac turned on the water and began to fill the water trough. "Did you propose it like a business arrangement or like you thought she should be honored? I'm curious how this went down."

"I told her I thought we should…"

Carson held up a hand. "You said it like that? You thought you *should* get married?"

"Not exactly like that. Look, she isn't going to marry me, that's all that matters. And it's probably wise of her to say no. I can't imagine I'd be much of a husband. Besides that,

I've never been one to stay in one place for very long."

"Or with one woman," Carson added.

Colt went after him, but Isaac stepped between the two of them, pushing Colt back with one hand while removing the toothpick with the other. He pointed the tiny weapon at Colt.

"I don't know what he said." Isaac pointed to his damaged ear. "But I'm sure he deserves whatever you were going to dole out. Keep in mind, you were hospitalized for almost two weeks, and he's in the best shape of his life."

"Thanks," Colt said. "Glad you pointed that out. And I don't need for *you* to point out my faults," he said to Carson. "I know them better than anyone."

"I'm sorry for getting under your skin," Carson said with a half grin. "Are you planning on seeing Jack this time?"

Of course they both knew he'd been in town. The last time he'd been here, he'd bought this property. The time before that, he'd only been in town long enough to lend Holly the money for the café.

"I planned on it," he said. "I'm going to be here for a while."

"He's in Tulsa for a day or two. I think

you're gonna be glad that you're here," Carson told him.

"Am I?" Colt asked. "I'm not so sure."

"Take it from me, you need to do this. You need to talk to Jack and finally put the past behind you," Carson informed him with the wisdom of an older brother. The kind of wisdom that got under Colt's skin. Or used to.

"I'll talk to him. I'll deal with the past."

"Good to hear," Isaac said. "And now I'm going home to my wife. I'd guess you have a lot to think about."

Isaac surprised him by giving him a quick hug. Carson did the same. Then they left, both climbing back into Isaac's truck.

For what it was worth, Colt thought that Isaac was right. He had a lot to think about. Mostly, who he was going to be now that he had a daughter, and now that he knew Holly's resentment hadn't lessened over time. He couldn't fault her for that. He didn't trust himself too much, either.

He was going to need God's help in becoming the man he knew he needed to be. A man who didn't walk out on the people he loved.

It was going to be a long road ahead.

Chapter Four

Holly heard Dixie coming down the stairs Saturday morning and her gut instantly tightened. They hadn't talked much the previous night. Instead they'd played a board game, watched some television and generally pretended the situation they found themselves in wasn't strange. It had been easier to ignore the reality that this might be temporary.

At bedtime she'd taken Dixie upstairs to a bedroom where a quilt Holly's grandmother had made covered the twin bed. The dresser had been painted white to match the eyelet curtains, and the window was open a crack, letting in a breeze and the sounds of the country night. Dixie had walked around the room, touching a music box with a dancing ballerina, then she'd looked out the window at the fields blanketed in silvery moonlight.

They'd talked as Dixie got ready for bed. Then Holly had tucked her daughter in, kissing her cheek and praying with her for the first time since that morning they'd given her to Becky. After tucking her in, Holly had stepped into the hall, closing the door behind her, and cried until she was dry.

This morning they would have real conversations about their lives, about the past and the future.

"Good morning," she said, pasting on a smile as Dixie came through the door, Opal's calico cat in her arms.

"Hi." Dixie became shy, burying her face in the neck of the cat. The ornery feline growled, then tried to escape. Dixie let her go. "She's not very friendly."

"She can be very moody. How did you sleep?"

Dixie shrugged. "I guess okay. There's a train somewhere."

"It's several miles away but on a clear night you can hear it like it's next door."

"Yeah, it was loud. Tulsa is loud, too. But it's a different loud. How did you sleep?" Dixie asked in return.

"I guess okay." They smiled at each other. "Pancakes?"

"Uh, no, thank you. I don't like them."

Holly looked at the griddle and the four pancakes. "I'm so sorry, next time I'll ask first."

"You can still eat them," Dixie offered.

"I don't like them, either." Holly laughed at the realization. "I just thought you might. But I also made bacon."

"We could have toast and bacon?" Dixie suggested.

"Good idea." Holly dropped some bread in the toaster.

"Where's Opal, I mean, my grandmother?" Dixie went after the cat, forgetting the near scratch that had caused her to let the animal free. "So odd. I don't know what to call everyone."

"I want you to call us whatever feels comfortable. You're in charge here, Dixie. At least as far as how we progress and what you choose to call us."

"You want me to stay here, don't you?" Dixie grabbed a slice of toast and a knife to spread peanut butter. "Can I have coffee?"

"Do you usually drink coffee?"

Dixie grinned. "Nope, but I thought I'd try."

"If you want to try coffee, you may." Holly

couldn't ignore the very serious question her daughter had asked. "And yes, I want you to stay here. I want you more than you could ever realize."

"But you didn't. Once." Hurt fueled the words making them painful to hear.

"I wanted you then. I want you now." She hooked her daughter's chin with her finger and turned her head so they were facing each other. "I have missed you every single day for eleven years. Giving you up was the hardest decision I've ever had to make. But I wanted you to have everything. I knew what bringing you here would mean for you. I was only nineteen, and I knew I wasn't ready to be a single mom. And Colt…"

She wasn't going to condemn him now, to their child. He needed to be her dad, her hero. He would have to earn it, but he deserved the opportunity.

Holly drew in a breath and continued. "Colt and I were a mess. We knew that Becky could give you love, stability, security. I knew in my heart that she was the best person to raise you."

Dixie took a bite of her toast. "So now you think you're ready to be a parent?" One dark brow arched.

"I don't know if anyone is ever really ready to be a parent."

"But you want me to stay here? With you?"

"I do. I really do." Holly meant it with all her heart, a heart that had been broken and still seemed to be missing pieces. And yet suddenly it felt more whole than ever before.

"I don't know what I want," Dixie said as she reached for the cup of coffee Holly had fixed for her. "I don't want to hurt your feelings. It's just my mom said to always be honest. Honesty builds understanding."

"I'm glad that's what she taught you." But it hurt, so much, to hear Dixie call someone else Mom. Holly swallowed the pain, forcing a smile. "Let's do something fun today. It's been a long time since I've taken a Saturday off."

"What do you want to do?"

"Find kittens," Opal said as she entered the room. She wore a housedress and was carrying a suitcase.

"Mom, what are you doing?"

Opal blinked and looked around. "I'm not sure. I thought I was going to the store."

"No, I'll go to the store."

Opal narrowed her eyes and studied Dixie. "Shouldn't Holly be in school?"

"I'm not Holly," Dixie blurted. "And I do need to be in school. But not today. Today is Saturday."

"Is it Saturday?" Opal sat her suitcase down. "Carson is coming to get me on Saturday."

"Mom, why would Carson be coming to get you?"

Opal was already sidetracked. Her attention turned to Dixie's hair. She smelled the dark tresses before lifting strands in her fingers. "You have the prettiest flowers."

Dixie's eyes widened. "Will she pull my hair?" she asked Holly.

Holly shook her head. "No, she won't. She meant hair, not flowers. Mom, sit down and I'll fix you breakfast. I have pancakes ready."

"Okay." But Opal stood in the center of the room, as if she wasn't sure which direction to turn.

Dixie took another sip of coffee, then she reached for Opal's hand. "Come on, Grandma Opal."

Holly watched Dixie lead her mother to the kitchen table. She should be doing that. The last thing she wanted was for her daughter to follow in her footsteps, taking on the role of caretaker. Holly had been Opal's caretaker for longer than she could remember.

Exhaustion hit her, suddenly draining her energy. She'd been going too long without real days off, always worrying about Opal because she knew it wasn't safe for her mother to be alone. On good days she took Opal to the café and gave her the job of rolling the flatware in napkins. Sometimes she gave her some dough to knead.

She knew, the way her mother knew, that it was reaching a time when they wouldn't be able to continue the charade that everything was fine. Pasting on a smile, she fixed her mother a plate and took it to the table. Opal smiled up at her as she cut the pancakes into bite-size pieces.

As Opal ate, Dixie and Holly sat at the table, sipping coffee and talking about their lives. Holly discussed the easy stuff, not the hard stuff like spending a large part of her life caring for her mom, nor the embarrassing stuff like being allowed to wear a unicorn costume for school pictures, or the painful stuff like not knowing her dad or having to take care of a mother who struggled with sobriety.

Dixie talked about growing up in Broken

Arrow, the large school she attended, her friends. And Daisy. It pained Holly to hear her daughter talk about the affection she felt for Colt's sister, Daisy, the woman who had been like a big sister but who had really been her aunt.

"I didn't know she was my aunt until…" Dixie bit down on her bottom lip. "Until my mom died. I should have known because our eyes are the same color."

"I'm sorry you didn't know."

Dixie shrugged. "It's okay, I guess. I mean, all of this is kind of weird."

"Yeah, kind of weird," Holly agreed.

After breakfast they cleaned up and then went outside to do what Opal suggested, search for kittens. Later they put away Dixie's clothes and the few trinkets she'd brought from home.

"I miss my stuff." She looked around the room. "It's a nice room but it doesn't feel like mine. Daisy has all my stuff."

"Well, if there's something you need, I can get it for you. Or if you want Daisy to send some of your things…"

Dixie shook her head. "No, that's okay. Right now I have enough."

They shared a look, both knowing what was left unsaid.

For a couple of months they were pretending to be the family they might have been. That meant Colt, front and center in Holly's life, filling a space he might have filled if…

If he hadn't cheated. If she'd known how to be the second half of a couple. If the two of them had made better choices.

Always if.

Colt didn't knock on the front door when he got to Holly's. He knew she'd stop him if he told her his plan. He parked his truck near the barn, got the Weed Eeater out of the back and headed for the fence row. The entire place needed attention, but he knew that this was a good place to start.

After he'd done a large section of the fence and was physically regretting it, he felt someone punching his arm.

He nearly swung the weed trimmer in her direction. "What are you doing sneaking up on me like that? That's a good way to get hurt."

She punched his arm a second time. "Yeah, well, this is a good way to get hurt, too. You do not have to do this. Actually, I don't want you to do this."

"It needs doing and you can't do everything. I mean, you can but not without wearing yourself into the ground."

"I do what needs to be done."

"I know you do."

She crossed her arms. "I'm not marrying you."

That took the wind out of his sails. "You already told me, but thanks for the reminder."

"I'm sorry, it's just…we don't have to pretend to be a couple, with you taking care of things for me around the house."

"I'm not."

She gave him a look.

"I'm not trying to force my way into your life or prove something to you," he said, wanting her to get it. "I want you to trust me. I want to be here, to be involved. She's our daughter. You're the mother of our daughter."

He wanted to be here. He'd never wanted to be anywhere, not really. Except when he was on the road, rescuing bull riders, sometimes playing the clown. He'd been running from his life for longer than he could remember. This had brought him to a stop, making him realize all the areas of his life that felt empty.

"She might not even want us." Her eyes watered and she dashed a hand across her cheeks. "I appreciate that you're willing to marry me in order to keep her, but she might pick Daisy, and then where would we be?"

"Married," he said without a smile, because in her current mood a smile might send her over the edge.

"Married and regretting a hasty decision."

"Ouch, that's kind of harsh."

"It's the truth and you know it." She exhaled but her gaze softened and she reached for his hand. "Oh, Colt, don't pretend you're suddenly a domesticated version of your former self. You're a bullfighter by trade and you spend a big portion of your year on the road. Are you suddenly going to quit your job?"

He hadn't given it a lot of thought. The doctor would okay him returning to work in six weeks. He hadn't planned anything beyond that.

She cocked her head and studied him. "Your silence speaks volumes. You're here temporarily. You brought her home and you thought your duty was done. You thought she'd pick me and that you'd stop by for the occasional visit."

"No one else makes me as mad as you," he growled at her.

"You're not my favorite person, either."

"At least we understand each other," he grumbled.

He took a step and stumbled as the muscles in his leg stiffened. Dropping the weed trimmer, he grabbed a fence post and drew in a deep breath as he tried to bear weight on his leg.

"Let me help you," she said, moving to his side, her arm sliding around his waist. "If you're doing this for attention, you're in big trouble."

He managed to laugh. "I can promise you, this is no act. But I think I can make it to the house."

"All right." She sounded less than sure. "I'm pretty certain you're not supposed to be doing manual labor yet."

"It's been a couple of months. I thought it would be fine."

With her help, he limped his way back to the house. Her arm remained around his waist and he couldn't help sniffing the floral scent of her hair.

"Stop," she hissed.

"My apologies." But he kept his nose there just a moment longer.

"You haven't changed at all."

"Not where you're concerned," he said. "But I'm determined not to hurt you again."

She shook her head and kept walking. As they did so, his muscles relaxed and with each step it got easier to move. He didn't remove her arm from his waist, or his arm from her shoulder. It felt too right, being so close to her. But it couldn't last forever. He sighed and put space between them.

"I can make it to the patio on my own."

"You sure?" Her dark eyes sought his, and he didn't know what the question pertained to, his health or something more.

"I'm sure." He collapsed on a chair on the patio.

"Is there something I can get you?" she asked as she sat in the chair across from his.

"No, I'm good. I just need to give it a minute."

"I'm putting the Weed Eater back in your truck." Holly jumped to her feet.

"I'll do it in a bit. Sit down and let's talk about your day."

She settled back into the chair. "It's been good. Me and Dixie talked all about our lives, parts of my life, all of hers. She asked if we were in love."

"What did you tell her?"

"I told her yes, that a long time ago we were in love."

The truth was, he still loved her. He thought he'd always loved her but eleven years ago he hadn't been the man she deserved. He'd taken her love and her trust and treated them as if they meant nothing.

It was something he regretted.

"Don't look at me like that," Holly said. The words brought him back to the present.

"Sorry, just lost in thought."

"I could tell." She leaned closer, the floral scent teasing his nose. "We'll figure this out without you falling on your sword."

"Falling on my sword?" He didn't understand.

"Marriage. The great sacrifice. I read through the papers. Becky didn't say we had to be married. Only that we have to provide a stable home life for our daughter. We can do that by sharing custody and coming up with an agreement on visitation. If she chooses us."

"Because you're worried about her relationship with Daisy. I know the two of them are close."

"I feel like the woman in the story of Solomon. I don't want to be the one who says to divide the baby. I don't want to be selfish and take Dixie from the life she knows."

"I know. We have her for two months, until the end of the school year. Let's agree that we won't keep her here if this isn't the life she wants."

He took Holly's hand and held it in his; her fingers devoid of jewelry. Her fingernails were blunt and unpainted. Then he lifted it to press a kiss against her palm.

"I'm sorry." He looked up, met her dark eyes with his. "I messed up but I'm going to do everything in my power not to hurt you this time."

"Colt…" Her eyes glistened and he wondered what she would say next.

But just then, the back door banged shut and he heard Dixie say something to Opal about kittens. He released Holly's hand and she settled back in her chair. With effort he got to his feet.

"Is it almost time for burgers?" he asked, needing something to do, some way to disrupt the tension.

"Almost. I'll make hamburger patties. You

have to clean the grill," she said with a forced smile.

Dixie rounded the corner and saw them. She came to a skittering halt. "Hey, there you are."

"Yes, here I am." He went over to her and gave her a quick hug.

"Why are you limping?" she asked.

"I was trying to help out with the lawn."

Her gray eyes widened. "You're not supposed to do that. You should sit down. Grandma and I will be back in a minute. We have to put the kitten back in the barn. Have you been in the barn? It's amazing. It's huge on the inside. There are birds that dive-bomb the cats. And they flew after me, too."

"That's not surprising." He walked with her, listening to her ramble on about kittens, birds and how maybe she could get a horse.

She was a novelty to him. He hadn't spent much time around kids; even his nieces and nephew were foreign little beings that he saw from time to time, but he hadn't built much of a relationship with them.

That had been a mistake.

This small person, she was amazing. She lit up as she talked about the barn and the kittens. She kept a hand on Opal while she expounded on the wonders of an aging barn that had seen better days probably a half century ago.

They were halfway to the barn when she stopped talking and walking. "You should go back and rest," she told him.

"I'm fine."

"Yeah, but you don't seem fine. I think you need to go sit down." She shot a look past him to the patio.

He glanced that way and realized she was giving him a strong hint.

"See what I mean?" she said. "You should go rest."

He saluted. "Will do."

He returned to the patio and Holly. "She sent me back," he told her. "Show me where the grill is, and I'll get started."

She stood up and headed for the front door. He followed her inside. "I don't want to disappoint her. She expects us to spend time together, I think."

She took hamburger meat out from the fridge and started shaping patties.

"I watch them together and I don't know how to do what has to be done. My mom, she's slipping away. It's happening so much faster than I thought it would."

"I know."

"And now we have Dixie, and I don't want her to become me, another young girl caring for the people who should be taking care of her." She dropped the last burger on a plate and turned on the kitchen faucet to wash her hands.

She sniffled and the sound undid him. He wrapped his arms around her from behind. She leaned back into his embrace.

"I make a habit of doing the wrong things. But I'm here. I want to help."

"Thank you." She reached for paper towels on a wooden spindle on the counter and tore one free to wipe her eyes. "I hate being emotional. I'm strong. I can do this."

He moved next to her so that they were side by side, their shoulders touching. "You can do anything you set your mind to."

"I can do all things through Christ who strengthens me?" she asked, knowing the answer. The verse, one she'd memorized years ago in Vacation Bible School, had never been forgotten.

"You can, and you will." He slipped his arm around her waist and she leaned into him. He wanted her there forever. "And I'll be here for you."

She looked out the window and he watched with her as Opal and Dixie played with the kitten, then Dixie carried it back inside the barn. Just as she'd described, the swallows came swooping down, chasing her back to the yard.

"She's having fun," he said.

"I know." She remained in the circle of his arm. "And my mom loves having her here. I promised my grandmother I'd always take care of my mother. I feel like putting her in the nursing home is betraying that promise."

"Maybe it's time to talk to Carson about options?" He longed to ask who took care of her. But he knew the answer. She took care of herself. Barely.

For a few months, it could be his job to take care of her. If she would allow it.

Chapter Five

Sunday morning Colt woke early and headed for Mercy Ranch. He'd gotten a text the previous evening from Isaac. His dad, Jack West, was home. It was time for Colt to take his prodigal self back to the ranch he'd been avoiding for the past twenty years. He headed up the paved drive with the sun still tingeing the eastern sky pink and orange.

The ranch, no longer an old farmhouse and tumbledown barn, took him by surprise. The old farmhouse was still there, still a part of the landscape. But a new home had been built, a great log structure with big windows. The stable was a big metal building with an attached arena. Jack had done well, rebuilding his family ranch so that it was better than before.

He parked near the barn and got out, to be greeted by a nearly perfect spring morning. The air was cool and crisp but with the promise of warmth. The grass was emerald green with a sprinkling of yellow dandelions. An Oklahoma spring.

As good as it felt to be back, he also had a lot of memories that weren't so good. The last thing he needed was a trip down memory lane.

Colt headed for the stable, a massive building with the name Mercy Ranch emblazoned above the door.

Mercy Ranch. The name said it all. His dad believed in mercy and forgiveness. Colt had a difficult time accepting the ranch of his childhood—poorly managed and falling apart— with this gleaming and modern horse facility.

Plus he could hardly believe that the Jack West he'd known was the same man described in magazines as a gentle, kindhearted philanthropist who wanted nothing more than to provide a place for wounded veterans to heal.

He guessed he and his father could both fit into the prodigal role. Both had been down some hard roads, made mistakes, had regrets.

As he walked the spotlessly clean center aisle, he pulled back in surprise. Jack was sitting on the seat of his walker, waiting. As Colt approached, Jack looked up, tremors obvious in his head and arms. Parkinson's was taking its toll.

"Good morning," Colt said as he came to a stop in front of his father.

"Good morning to you, too." Jack grabbed the handles of the walker and pushed himself to his feet. "It's been a long time."

"Twenty years." Colt felt every single one of those years and he saw them in the lines of his dad's weathered face.

Colt held out a hand for his father to shake. It seemed like the right way to start. Jack took a step closer and gave him a hug instead, his arms trembling all the while. Colt stood there for a moment, unsure, then he put his arms around his dad.

"I'm glad you're here." Jack's voice wavered as he sat heavily on the seat of the walker. "How long will you be in town?"

"I'll be here for a good six weeks or so. I need to finish healing up, and I need to help Holly get settled with Dixie." Colt took a seat on the bench next to his father.

"I—" Jack stopped himself and merely shrugged. "There's coffee."

"That isn't what you were going to say."

"No, but I reckon I don't have the right to give advice."

"I think you're probably right about that." Colt leaned back against the wall behind him. "This isn't the way I want the conversation to go."

"No," Jack said. "I think we have plenty to talk about, but tearing chunks out of each other isn't going to fix anything. I know I don't have a right to interfere, but I do know a thing or two about making mistakes."

"I agree with that," Colt managed to say with humor in his voice.

"I'm sorry," Jack spoke softly, his voice raspy. "I hope someday you can forgive me."

Colt nodded.

When he'd been in the hospital, facing an unknown future, he'd had time to think about his life. With a tube down his throat for the better part of forty-eight hours, he'd spent time talking to the only one who could hear him: God.

He had continued the conversations even after he'd gotten out of the hospital. Those talks with his maker had been long overdue. He'd come to terms with his life, the mistakes he'd made and the people he'd hurt. Holly had been at the top of the list.

The conversations had included the relationship with his parents. Jack had been a broken man when he'd returned from Vietnam. He'd had brief moments of being the best dad around, alternating with moments of being the worst. After Colt's mother had left Jack and taken him and Carson and Daisy with her, Isaac had moved in. For some reason, Isaac's arrival had brought about change. Or maybe his wife leaving had started the changes.

"I forgive you," Colt said. The words were long overdue.

"Thank you." Jack's head shook as he looked at Colt. "I'm glad you came home."

"It isn't my home anymore," Colt said. "It's just another stopping place."

"Maybe," Jack said. "Maybe not. Life has a way of changing when we least expect. I know you have plans, but make sure you're following God's plans, too."

"I'm not sure if I'm ready for theological discussions with you."

Jack laughed a little. "Too soon?"

"Yeah. Let's work up to fatherly advice."

"You're a dad, too. Soon you'll be doling out your own fatherly advice from time to time. Sometimes it will be solicited and sometimes you'll just give it."

Colt jolted at the word *dad*. He hadn't spent a lot of time thinking of himself that way. *Dad*. The word meant something. It required something of him. For eleven years he hadn't been anyone's dad. Dixie had been Becky's child in every way that counted.

"When do I meet my granddaughter?" Jack asked, breaking through the silence.

"At church today. I'm going to pick them up."

Jack pushed himself to his feet. "I'll expect you all for lunch, so make sure you give Holly the invite. Opal is welcome, too. Maria is making pork tenderloin."

Maria ran the house at Mercy Ranch and was possibly the love of his father's life, if rumors were to be believed.

"We'll be here."

"I'm glad. I've got all three of my boys close by. It feels good. Now if I can only find a way to bring Daisy back."

"That'll be between you and Daisy," Colt said.

Colt watched the once tall and powerful Jack West make his way slowly down the aisle and out the door of the stable. He paused from time to time to rest but didn't quit. He had truly reinvented himself. He was the man everyone said he was: calm and quiet and thoughtful. A father a man could be proud of, but definitely not the father Colt had grown up with.

Colt had to figure out for himself what the word *father* meant for him and Dixie. He didn't want to just be the person who picked her up and dropped her off with Holly.

He didn't want to be the one who let her down.

No, he wanted to be the man who was there to make sure the boys behaved when they took her on a date. He wanted to be the man who made sure she knew her worth.

He wanted to take her to church, someday walk her down the aisle, all of the things a father did for his daughter.

A few minutes later he headed down the road toward Holly's farmhouse at the edge of town. When he pulled up to the house he spotted Holly on the patio, a cup of coffee on the table in front of her. She glanced up, frowning when she realized it was him.

She didn't get up to greet him. Instead she just sat there as he parked, headed her way and sat down across from her.

"What are you doing here?" she finally asked.

"I'm here to…" He cleared his throat, finding it harder to say the words than he'd imagined. "I'm here to be a dad."

"Oh, okay." She blinked, clearly puzzled.

"I want to take my daughter to church. I thought we might go as a family."

"A family."

"I know this is unexpected." He pulled a chair up next to hers. "I saw Jack today. He'd like for us to join them for lunch at the ranch."

"That is unexpected," she agreed. "It isn't that I don't want to go. I'm just not sure how to take Opal to church. I have a lot of memories of going as a child, not all of them good ones. Opal didn't always make life easy."

"I know." He got it. At times their childhood issues had run parallel. Her mother had been addicted to pills. His father had been an alcoholic. Neither of them had the best childhood memories.

She let out a jagged sigh. "I can do this. I'm an adult. I'm the mother. It's just not easy to suddenly put on the hat and remember that it isn't about me."

"You're the least selfish person I know, Holly. Even the adoption came about not because you were selfish. It was because you were *selfless*, choosing what you thought was best for her."

Holly remained silent for a moment, then said, "I'll get us all ready but it might take a few minutes." She pushed her chair back from the table but her expression had grown serious. "We can be friends, Colt. But that's all I can give you right now."

"I understand." That was probably for the best. He should have told her that he'd rethought his proposal. He had his own set of fears. What if he let them down, her and Dixie? What if he couldn't be the dad his daughter needed, or the man Holly needed?

One step at a time.

Holly had never seen herself as a coward but as they pulled up to the Hope Community Church, she felt an awful tightening in her gut and a real desire to run in the opposite direction. It made no sense, because she loved this church and the people who attended. She always volunteered when they had special events. And she did her best to support her community.

But showing up today with Colt, Dixie and her mother was a lot. On any normal day she could walk through the doors and greet everyone with a smile. She might have once been "that poor little Carter girl," but now she was a respected business owner. People grew up and overcame their pasts.

Except today her past had come to church with her. And Opal had woken up in her own version of the past, unsure of who Holly was and convinced that Dixie was her daughter.

Colt parked, and the four of them sat in his truck for a few minutes. That's when she realized he was nervous as well. He tossed her a quick look as he pulled the keys from the ignition.

"Second thoughts?" she asked.

"And thirds and fourths." He grinned, as if that smile would convince her he was fine.

"Are we getting out?" Dixie asked, leaning over the seat.

"We are definitely getting out."

"Are you chicken?" she continued. "I mean, here we are. What do we call ourselves? The Carter-Wests?"

"You're making this more difficult." Colt shot her a look over his shoulder.

"I'm trying to keep the mood light." She reached for the door handle and climbed out, helping Opal down and leaving them to follow.

"She takes the bull by the horns, doesn't

she?" Colt said it as a matter of pride. "A lot like her ol' dad."

"Oh, please," Holly said. "You'd turn tail and run if she weren't already out of the truck."

He laughed and she wasn't about to admit that running had been on her mind, too. His laughter eased something inside her, making her feel more comfortable in the moment. She'd missed their friendship, even though it had been years since they'd truly been friends. During their difficult childhoods, they'd been each other's support.

"I missed you," she admitted as she got out of the truck. He was still behind the wheel and she stood there looking in at him, trying to figure out the crazy swirl of conflicting emotions that made her want him as a best friend, yet told her to guard her heart against him.

But he couldn't have her heart. He'd already broken it once. There was no way she'd let him do it again. She made a quick search, saw Dixie and her mother nearing the church entrance. Isaac and his wife, Rebecca, were with them.

"I forgive you," she said as he started to slide out of his seat. He stopped and gave her his full attention. "I've needed to say those words for a long time. I prayed I could forgive you and I've worked on it, but I think I need to say it out loud in order to make it real. I need to say this so we can find a way to raise Dixie together. I forgive you for hurting me. And you did hurt me. I loved you. I trusted you. But that's in the past. Today we have to find something to build on for Dixie."

"I'm going to do my best for you both, Holly."

"I know."

It wasn't perfect, but it was a starting point.

They walked toward the church together. The slow walk gave people time to look their way, whisper, speculate. She scanned the crowd, spying her mother first, standing with Carson and Kylie West. Then she focused on Dixie, who seemed to have found a friend in Rebecca West's daughter, Allie.

Holly reached for Colt's hand and gave it a squeeze.

"You okay?" he asked.

"I'm okay. I just wanted to say thank you, for bringing her here."

The church bells rang, keeping him from responding, and she was thankful. The sound of the bells carried across the countryside.

Cars were still pulling into the parking lot. Families walked up the steps together and entered the building that had been a fixture in Hope for more than one hundred years. Dixie hurried to Holly's side, taking hold of her hand.

Together they walked up the steps, the four of them, an odd, makeshift family. Once inside the church, they were joined by the West family. Holly was taken aback by the way the family circled them, drawing them in with hugs and warmth.

For a woman who had spent most of her life on the outside of such circles, it was overwhelming and more than a little uncomfortable. Holly moved to the side as Colt's family made a fuss over Dixie. They hugged her, laughed as she told them funny stories. Like Colt, she knew how to charm people. A skill Holly had never developed.

"How are you doing?" Kylie West, Carson's wife, asked as she sidled up to Holly.

"I'm good." She smiled as she said it.

Kylie gave her a long look. "Of course you are. I mean, this can't be easy, right? Having your child show up…"

Holly interrupted. "It's absolutely the best thing that could have happened."

"Of course it is," Kylie continued in her therapist voice that Holly knew well.

"It was a shock but I'm not at all sorry that she's here."

"Colt, on the other hand…" Kylie teased, putting her friend hat on once again.

"He's a trial," she agreed. Just then, he glanced her way, winking as he flashed her his dimpled half grin. He'd left his cowboy hat in the truck and his dark hair was slightly messy.

"Yes, a trial. That's how I would categorize the West men, trials. They will try your patience, try your heart, try you every which way."

Kylie had been Carson's childhood sweetheart and when he'd returned to Hope, a widower with two small children, the two had reconnected. And fallen in love all over again.

Holly wanted to tell her friend that even though it had worked out well for Kylie and Carson, she and Colt were not going down that road. Holly knew all too well that Colt had wandering eyes and feet. He wouldn't stay put for long. And the idea of losing him again wasn't something she wanted to think about.

Today wasn't about him; it was about finding the best way to build a relationship with Dixie.

Fortunately, Pastor Stevens had stepped behind the pulpit, signaling the beginning of services. Holly found her mother sitting with Jack and Maria. The pew behind them had been left open for the remainder of the large West clan. Holly slid in next to Dixie, and then Colt was there, next to her.

She had memories of the two of them as children in this church. Colt was definitely no longer a boy of eleven with toads in his pockets and dirt-smudged cheeks. As much as she wanted to deny there could be anything between them, it mattered that he was there next to her as they attended church together as a family.

It mattered that he reached for her hand.

To her heart, it all mattered, even though her brain knew better. Warning sirens were going off, telling her to take shelter.

She chose to ignore them.

Chapter Six

Colt had been in a lot of churches over the years, big cathedrals, storefront gatherings, large arenas and even cowboy churches located outdoors. This church in his hometown still spoke to his heart in ways that no other church could. Sitting in here with his family made it all the more real for him.

Sitting next to Holly shook him in ways he hadn't expected. It felt like the place he was meant to be, and the place he shouldn't be.

At the end of the service he bowed his head with everyone else. He prayed to be the father Dixie needed. He prayed he wouldn't let her or Holly down. *Lord, let me be a better man.*

All around him people were standing, moving down the aisle to leave. Holly stared at him as if she thought he'd lost his mind. He winked at her, grabbing hold of the pew in front of him to push himself to his feet.

"Why do you do it?" she asked.

He grabbed his cane and stepped into the aisle so she could join him.

"Fight bulls, I mean," she added. Dixie slid out of their pew but didn't stay with them. She headed for the front door, where his family—her family—stood waiting.

He'd brought her here and given her probably the best gift he could give a kid. Family. A real family with aunts, uncles and cousins.

"Why do I fight bulls?" he repeated. "I guess I do it for the adrenaline rush." He shrugged as he answered. "And because I like knowing that I've kept those guys safe. I worry about them when I'm not in the arena. I know the other bullfighters take the job just as seriously as I do, but it's like leaving my kids at day care. You know they're going to be cared for but you want to be the one doing it."

"How noble of you." Isaac appeared at their side.

"Would it be noble if I rearranged your face?" Colt asked.

"It would be wrong to hit your brother in church. Besides, I'm already wounded." Isaac pointed to the scar from the explosion that had stolen the hearing in his left ear.

"You surely had something else to say since you came looking for us," Colt responded.

"I thought I'd remind you both that the family gets together at Mercy Ranch for lunch on Sunday. It's the one time of the week we're all guaranteed to be together."

They walked toward the doors together, but Colt saw the hesitation in Holly's face.

"I should take Opal home. This has been a lot for her and she doesn't do well in places that are unfamiliar," she said softly, casting a worried glance in her mother's direction.

Opal had extricated herself from Holly's hold and walked down the steps ahead of them. Colt reached for the rail and eased himself down slowly, first one leg, then the other.

"Hard to maneuver when you're missing some muscle, isn't it?" Isaac asked as he waited for Colt.

"It's getting better. Physical therapy and exercises to build it back up. It won't ever be the same, but it'll be good enough."

"Kind of like you?" Isaac asked with a grin.

"Yeah, I guess." He let his gaze trail after Holly like a coon dog in hunting season. "I'll talk to Holly about lunch."

"It would do her good."

"I know," Colt responded as he took a step to put distance between himself and his overbearing sibling.

"You all coming to the ranch for lunch?" Carson caught him as he headed for Holly and Dixie. God save him from interfering brothers! That should have been his prayer. Carson's wife Kylie and his two children were close behind. Maggie, Carson's daughter, spotted him and ran as fast as her little legs could carry her.

"Uncle Colt!" She flew at him and he picked her up, hugging her tight. He liked to believe he'd helped Carson and Kylie find each other and thus a family was made.

Sometimes he managed to do the right thing.

"Hey, Princess, how's life?"

"I got a pony!" She hugged his neck as she told him. "And I named it Goldie because she's…"

"Gold?"

She laughed. "No, silly, she's spotted. But she's worth a lot."

Next to him Holly laughed, a real honest-to-goodness laugh. He found the sound contagious. For a moment the past, the heartache, his failures—all were forgotten as Maggie told them about the black-and-white pony and how she could jump a whole foot with her on her back.

"Okay, let's get everyone rounded up and head out to the ranch." Carson reached for his daughter. "You are very full of yourself today."

"I'm full of myself every day." She laughed as she made the pronouncement. "That's what Grandpa Jack says."

"It is indeed what he says," Carson acknowledged. "See you all there?"

"Yes, see you there," Colt agreed. And just like that, they were all one big happy family and no one mentioned the elephant in the room—that they'd never been a happy family before.

He gathered up what had become his temporary family—Holly, Dixie and Opal. For the time being they were his, and watching over them meant he had less time to think about a Sunday family lunch with Jack. He had less time to think about their futures, which were precarious at best.

"Are you okay?" Holly asked after he'd helped her mother and Dixie into the back seat of his truck, then moved to open her door.

Jack hadn't done much right as a father, but he had taught his sons to pitch a curveball, work hard and open the door for a woman. He guessed those things had served Colt well. He'd gotten a college baseball scholarship, could face down some of the meanest bulls on the planet, and he could stand next to Holly, and just soak up her goodness. Maybe some of it would rub off on him?

"I'm good." He cleared his throat to pretend he hadn't been woolgathering.

"Liar," she whispered.

Her dark eyes sought his. They asked questions. He didn't give a lot of answers. He didn't share his story with just anyone. But he and Holly? They knew each other's stories. They'd lived through them, together.

"Lunch with Jack," he admitted. "That's something I hadn't ever planned on. Ever again."

"You don't have to do it for us," she insisted. "We can go to my place and have bologna sandwiches."

"Tempting," he said.

He was tempted to brush a strand of her windblown hair behind her ear. He was tempted to admit a lot of feelings that would probably overwhelm them both. He knew better than to do that.

Be the tortoise, not the hare. That had to be his mantra. Because when he finally claimed her heart, he would be someone she could count on to keep her safe. Someone who wouldn't let her down.

"So?" she prodded.

"I have to go there," he said. "And see that he's changed. I have to give our daughter a chance to know her family."

"Give yourself a chance to know your father as more than the man who left scars?" she asked.

"Yes, that, too."

He wondered if she thought of him when she said that. Would she ever give him a chance to be more? As she got in his truck and he closed the door, he had hope.

Holly didn't want to admit it, but she had her own case of nerves as they pulled up to the main house at Mercy Ranch. These people were her friends, she reminded herself. Or as close as she got to friends. She'd never been one to engage in small talk, or to share much about her life. People who were close to her understood.

The café had become her social place, bringing her into the lives of her customers. She was Millie's granddaughter, Opal's daughter. People asked how she was doing. They asked about her mother. Few of them pushed too deeply for answers.

With Dixie in her life, she lost that anonymity. It also meant Colt was here, with her, with his family. As they walked toward the front of the house she noticed him fidgeting with his hat. She saw his easy smile for Dixie and heard him softly asking her mother if she was doing okay.

She spied a grimace on his face as he leaned a little more on the cane that she knew he didn't like to use. She guessed the idea of falling appealed less than the idea of looking weak. It was temporary, he'd told her.

She knew all about temporary.

As they approached the house Dixie reached for her hand. Holly glanced down at their joined hands, and over Dixie's head she met Colt's eyes. He winked and nodded, just barely. Everything about this moment unsettled her. Dixie holding her hand, Colt helping her mother up the stairs. The four of them, together.

She wanted it so much. She'd never wanted anything more.

At the front door they drew to a halt. Colt raised his hand to knock but froze. He leaned heavily on his cane and stared off at some distant point on the horizon. She followed his gaze to where it landed on the two-story farmhouse a good distance away. Colt had spent his childhood in that home, which now served as a residence for men, wounded veterans, who lived on Mercy Ranch.

"The two of you acting all tense sure isn't helping things any," Dixie spoke softly as they stood there, waiting. "This place is humungous. No one warned me that Jack West had a home like this."

Colt grinned. "You're right. I'm sorry."

"I get it," Dixie continued. "I mean, I just recently met my parents so I can kind of relate. I guess we're both getting to know our dads."

Colt looked as if he might cry. Holly felt tears sting the back of her eyes and she drew in a painful breath.

Colt pulled Dixie close and kissed the top of her head in an affectionate way that Holly could only describe as fatherly. He had that way about him. He could easily slide into any role and make it look easy. Even fatherhood.

Holly envied him that because she felt like she was wading in quicksand trying to figure out how to be the mother Dixie needed. She didn't want to move too quickly or hold back in her usual way. She wanted Dixie to know she was there for her.

"I know you understand," Colt told their daughter. "You're handling it like a pro."

"Are you nervous about spending time with Grandpa Jack? Aunt Daisy won't come and visit him. I heard her talking with my…" Her expression crumpled and she suddenly wiped her nose on her sleeve and struggled to manage a smile. "He was very nice at church."

Colt looked to Holly for help. She gave her a brief hug. "I'm sorry."

"I know," Dixie said. "Everyone is sorry but…" She sniffled again. "I do miss her and I'm not sure what's gonna happen."

Holly kept her arm around Dixie. "What happens is we are all going to do our best to make sure you're happy and you know you're loved." And then she said the second-most-difficult words of her life. "And if you choose to live with Daisy instead of us, we will support that."

"Do you want me?" The question seemed painful for everyone. Even Opal, who suddenly seemed aware and reached for her granddaughter.

"We all want you," Opal assured her. "Holly wants you. She always has. If it hadn't been for Colt West…"

Colt chuckled. "I'm right here, Opal."

She narrowed her eyes at him. "Nope."

Dixie stepped forward, her hand raised. "Do we knock or go on in? I mean, I guess if we're family we just walk in, right?"

Colt pushed the door open. "After you, ladies."

They walked through the foyer into the living room, a vast space with large windows, leather furniture arranged around a fireplace and a couple of cushioned rocking chairs facing the windows.

"This is lovely," Opal said, pausing in the middle of the room. "I do think I'm going to just sit down for a bit."

"You're sure?" Holly asked. "Mom, I can take you home."

"I'm not going home." Opal sat in a nearby recliner. "You all go on and I'll be here."

Colt grabbed a quilt off one of the rocking chairs and placed it over her. "Yell if you need us."

She was already closing her eyes but she nodded.

Holly paused in the doorway, but Colt urged her on.

"She's okay, she's just tired," he assured her.

"I know, I just have to know that she's okay. We should lock the front door. She's never wandered away but I'm afraid she might. There are nights I get up three or four times to check on her, just making sure she's still in her room asleep."

"You need to let people help," he told her. "Let me help you. I can't do much but I can watch over Opal."

"I let people help," she began, but he gave her a look that stopped her. "Okay, I'm not the best at asking for help. But she's *my* responsibility."

They walked through the house together and when they reached the kitchen they were greeted by a swarm of family and ranch residents. The kitchen, dining room and family room were all one large area, and off the family room was a breakfast nook. It made for an open gathering place for a very large group of people.

A serving table had been set up with warming trays. A few people stood in line to serve themselves. Others were already seated with their food. Jack saw them enter and headed toward them, a large smile on his face, more likely directed at Dixie than at either of them.

When he stood a few feet away, his expression softened. He maneuvered his walker to the side and stood a little taller.

"I'm so glad to have you here. I now have all of my grandchildren under this roof."

"But not—" Dixie caught herself as the words slipped out.

"Not what?" Jack asked, confusion furrowing his brow.

"Not a day went by when I didn't think about having a family."

Dixie smiled up at her grandfather, then she took Colt's hand as if it were a lifeline. Father and daughter stood together in that moment, facing their past and their present. Maybe their futures.

Holly's heart shifted, like sand with the changing tide. It fell apart just a little but got rearranged in a whole new way.

"How're you doing? You okay?" Kylie asked, coming to stand next to Holly.

"I am. I'm good."

Kylie handed her a plate. "Go get some food."

"I don't know if I can eat, but I'll get my mother a plate."

"Where's Opal?"

"She's in the living room, resting."

Kylie walked with her toward the food. "I'll get your mom a plate and you get your own."

"I had a break yesterday," Holly told her. "Stacy took over at the café. I stayed home with Dixie."

Kylie picked up a piece of chicken. "Will your mom eat this?"

Holly shrugged. "She might eat it. To be honest, I think she's forgetting to eat. Or maybe forgetting how to eat. There are days when I cut her food up and feed her, just to make sure."

"Holly, you need more help. Or you might have to accept that it's time to put Opal somewhere where she can get the care she needs. And I want you to know, we'll all be here to help you."

Holly was silent for a moment, then said, "I appreciate that."

Kylie studied her. "I haven't talked to Colt and I don't think he's shared much with Carson. Is he staying? I mean, the three of you…"

Kylie shrugged. "I'm sorry, that isn't any of my business. I just think that you look happier and I'm sure that's because Dixie is here."

Dixie, the child that Kylie and most of Holly's friends never knew existed. Now she was here. And Colt was here. Everything was different.

The three of them trying to be a family—it was something Holly had dreamed of twelve years ago, until Colt had broken her heart and she'd faced the reality that she couldn't raise a baby on her own. She'd been afraid, overwhelmed, and had made the toughest decision ever: to give her baby up for adoption.

"It's been an amazing couple of days," Holly admitted. "And frightening, because it's a big change for all of us."

Kylie touched her arm. "Today isn't the day for long talks. But maybe soon, over coffee?"

Holly started to respond but Dixie appeared at her side. She'd overheard the conversation. Kylie excused herself, telling Holly she would make sure Opal ate.

Holly lifted a piece of pork and offered it to her daughter. "Pork or chicken?"

Dixie shrugged, raising her eyes to meet Holly's. "Do you regret that I'm here? Am I going to make things too hard for you?"

Holly fought back tears. "I want you. I want you more than anything. We will figure this out. And I promise, it's actually the best thing ever, having you here. But I don't know the little things. Like what you like to eat for lunch. I want to know everything."

Dixie leaned over and reached for some asparagus with a fork. "I like asparagus."

"Do you?" Holly asked, almost afraid to breathe. "So do I. It's my favorite. You never answered, pork or chicken?"

"Neither, really. I guess chicken better than pork. I like beef. A lot."

"Me, too," Holly said, smiling at her daughter.

"I also like coffee but I don't want to drink yours because I don't know if it will make you mad."

"It won't make me mad. Not at all. I'll make a full pot in the mornings so that there's enough for you to have a cup." Holly looked at the food on the table. "What about potatoes?"

"I don't like sweet potatoes," Dixie leaned to look in the warmer. "I do like mashed with bacon."

"Me, too," Holly said, joy bubbling up in an embarrassing way. "And I don't like sweet potatoes, either."

At that revelation Dixie beamed.

Suddenly Colt's spicy male scent wafted in Holly's nose, taking her by surprise. In a good way. He hovered at her shoulder and surveyed the potatoes.

"In case anyone was wondering, I happen to like sweet potatoes," he informed them. "And chicken."

"You're definitely odd man out," Dixie said with a smirk. "Voted off. No longer on the island."

He put a hand to his heart. "Anything but that."

"Sorry!" Dixie informed him with a grin. "Sweet potatoes are an automatic disqualification."

"Ouch. For that, I'm eating all the mashed potatoes. And you have to eat chicken."

"No way." She looked at both of them. "I know the two of you probably want to sit with me. And I'm okay with that. But would it be okay if I go sit with Allie? She has a horse and she told me I can ride it."

"Go ahead," Holly told her.

With a grin Dixie was off to join her cousin. Allie hadn't been in the family long. She'd come to Hope with her mother, Rebecca. And then Rebecca had met Isaac and a family had been born.

"We're going to be okay, you know, and so is she."

"We didn't believe we could do it eleven years ago. What makes you think we can do it now?"

"We're in a much different place than we were back then. We've both grown up and I think we're both responsible adults. We'll do this. For her. We can build a friendship." He gave her an earnest look. "Trust me."

Trust. That was the part where their relationship always broke down. For Dixie's sake she wanted to—needed to—trust him.

Her heart wanted to believe it could happen. But her head…not so much.

Chapter Seven

On Monday morning, Colt knocked on Holly's door. He could hear what sounded like chaos inside. Someone running. Someone else yelling about a backpack. He knocked again and Opal appeared. She looked at him through the window of the locked door.

"Opal, please let me in."

She shook her head.

"Opal, I need to help Holly."

"She's going to school," Opal yelled through the door.

He knocked a third time, then he pulled out his phone and called Holly. She answered, breathless.

"Opal won't let me in in the house. I'm here to help get Dixie ready for school."

"Really? Because you know what shoes go

with skinny jeans and which top will make her look cool and which one makes her look like a loser?"

Holly opened the door, her hair in a messy bun that probably hadn't started out as such.

"Come in, because if you think you can handle this, have at it." She motioned him inside. "She's in the living room. Wailing."

"I'm not wailing," Dixie called from the front of the house. "I can't go to school my first day looking like a loser. I get that you wore a unicorn costume for picture day, but I'm not that..." She paused. "Brave."

Entering the living room, Colt saw that Dixie had three pairs of shoes on the floor in front of her, two tops in her hand, and her hair was sticking out in all directions. Colt wasn't an expert but he was pretty sure they were going to be late for her first day of school.

"Don't look at me like that!" Dixie hid her face in a throw pillow she grabbed off the couch.

"I'm sorry." He looked at the clothing, then said, "I think the tan sneakers and the pink shirt."

She looked at them, then held them together. She held the shirt up to her body and slipped a foot in the shoe.

"You think?"

"Yeah, I think." He winked at Holly.

She didn't look amused. He guessed if he'd been arguing with a preteen about clothing, he wouldn't be in the best mood, either.

"I don't know…" Dixie began.

"You know that outfit is as good as any," he told her, taking her by the shoulders and guiding her to the stairs. "Get up there and get dressed. Being on time is important."

She huffed at that. "What if no one likes me?"

"Everyone will like you, I promise, and you're going to look great," he encouraged. "But you have to get there first."

"Right." Finally, she stomped up the stairs.

Holly sighed loudly, then sat down on the bench in the foyer. "That was exhausting. And as much as I appreciate your help, I'm a little miffed that you could swoop in, pick an outfit and have her upstairs in five minutes."

"I have some skills."

"Mmm-hmm. I already told her that outfit was good."

He pulled her into his arms and she went willingly.

"It's going to work out. I promise."

"Is it?" she asked. "I want it to. I want her

more than I can even put into words. But I don't know if she wants me. And I don't know if I'm good for her. I'm so tired and I had to leave the café mid-breakfast rush in order to get here and wake her up."

"I'm sorry. I should have been here to help."

She looked up at him, her expression unsettled. But as he rubbed her back she put her head against his shoulder. He stroked her hair and after a moment she gazed up into his eyes.

Slowly he lowered his head and touched his lips to hers. At first she was still, but then her hands moved from his shoulders to his neck. She kissed him back, her lips brushing his.

Just then, they heard a door slam and then someone running. He heard Dixie make a gagging noise.

"No PDA," she called out from the top of the stairs. "I'm young and impressionable."

"We're your parents," Colt informed her.

"Yeah, but…that's just not okay. I don't want to see that."

Even though Holly had turned bright red, she laughed and Colt felt a wave of relief. She was okay. They weren't falling apart. She wasn't pushing him away. She might not have noticed, but she'd remained in his arms.

Dixie came down the stairs, a backpack over her shoulder, her dark hair in a braid. "I'm not going to be late."

"No, you're not." Holly herded her to the back door.

"What about Grandma Opal?" Dixie asked as they went out the back door.

"I'll check on her," Holly promised. "I try to come home several times a day."

"Will she be safe by herself?" Dixie asked they headed for Colt's truck.

"She'll be fine. She's used to this routine." Holly had her keys out and Colt didn't know how to stop her or if he should.

"Can't we all go together?" Dixie asked, taking care of the situation for him.

Holly looked from her car to his truck. "I suppose we can go together."

They climbed in his pickup and headed towards school. Dixie jabbered for the first few minutes, then she was silent.

"What if no one likes me?" she whispered.

"They'll like you," he told her. "Give them time. Give it a chance."

He glanced in his rearview mirror. She made quick eye contact with him and looked away.

"I miss my friends," she admitted. "I didn't

tell them goodbye. But they might wonder where I'm at."

"I think Daisy probably took care of things," Colt told her. "But we can get numbers and you can call your friends."

"I miss Daisy, too." Then there was silence again. He saw her swipe at a tear sliding down her cheek. Another followed.

Holly half turned in her seat. "We can call Daisy. Maybe she could come see you or we could go visit her. And pick up some of your stuff that you're missing."

Dixie nodded. "I'd like that. I don't think she would come, and she has the twins."

"Twins?" Holly choked on the word. "What?"

Colt sighed. Dixie sighed.

"I'm not good at keeping secrets," Dixie said.

Colt agreed with that. "It's hard to do."

"Should you all tell me something?"

"We can't." Dixie spoke softly. "I'm sorry. It's just that… Daisy made me promise."

"Of course." Holly gave him a look and he shrugged. He'd made the same promise.

He pulled up in front of the school. "Here we are."

"Here we are," Dixie said a little too happily.

"Yes," Holly repeated. "Here we are. Saved by the bell."

He parked and they walked together into the school. Dixie stayed between them and he thought he heard her teeth clenching.

"It's okay," he told her. "Really."

"Easy for you to say," she muttered.

"I had to change schools when I wasn't much older than you. My mom left my dad and we headed to Texas. We never came back."

"You never saw your dad again?"

He shook his head. "Not until recently."

"I can't imagine not seeing you again. Even if I live with Daisy, I would still want to see you."

Holly's face fell. Dixie must have noticed because she gave a bright smile.

"I would want to see you *both*," she said.

"The point is," he said. "Going to a new school can be scary, but it can also be a good experience. You'll make new friends, maybe learn new things, try new activities."

"I guess." She shifted her backpack to her other shoulder. "Like maybe volleyball. I wanted to play but there were a lot of girls on the team. We couldn't all play."

"We can check into volleyball," Holly assured her.

And just like that, they were doing the parent thing. It felt good. Maybe better than good. They entered the school office together and filled out some paperwork. Holly told her she could come over to the café after school.

Normal parent stuff.

Then they had to leave her, because that's what parents did. Colt didn't want to tell her goodbye or leave her with strangers.

Holly took his hand. "Come on, she'll be fine. If there are any problems, they'll call us."

He wasn't so sure about that. "Do they have our numbers? Maybe we should have gotten her a cell phone. What about lunch?"

Holly led him out the front door. She hugged him tight and he knew that the dampness on his shirt came from her tears. She wasn't as tough as she'd let on.

"We did it," she blubbered. "Oh wow, I can't imagine what kindergarten would have been like."

He wanted to imagine it. In his mind, he saw a boy with dark hair and dark eyes with his mother's sweetness. The desire to have that dream became a living thing in his mind.

What did Holly dream about? Did she think about them as a family, having more children, doing this parenting thing together? Or was she content with the way things were between them, co-parenting, him on the road part of the year?

He'd never considered himself to be a coward but when it came to knowing the truth about her feelings, he didn't have the courage to ask.

Not yet.

There were several police cars in front of the café. Officers were gathered in a group. Carson West stood with them.

And then she saw her mother.

"Colt, they have my mom." As soon as the truck slowed to a stop, she jumped out and ran, leaving him to figure it out for himself.

"Holly, she's fine," Carson said, taking her by the arm.

"What is she doing here?" She tugged away from him and hurried to her mother's side. "Mom, are you okay?"

Opal was clearly confused. "I couldn't find the school but I knew I had to pick you up."

"No, Mom, I took Dixie to school. Remember?"

"No, I don't think that's it." Opal let out a long sigh and shook her head. "I just don't know."

"I can take her home now." She put an arm around her mother's waist but knew as she looked from Carson to the officers that she wasn't taking her mom home again. Ever.

Colt limped toward them, and oh, how she needed him there. She didn't want to, but she couldn't help it. She didn't know why her heart would pick the person who had broken her and would more than likely do it again, but right now, she needed him.

"Holly." One of the officers, a regular, cleared his throat. "Miss Carter, we found your mom walking along the highway outside of town. She was clearly confused. We asked her for an address so we could take her home but she couldn't remember."

Tears fell, hot and salty, down her cheeks. She swiped at them, angry for the weakness, angry that she hadn't done better. She put her hands on her mother's cheeks and looked deep into dark eyes, wanting to see recognition.

"Mom." She whispered it again. Opal gave her a sympathetic look.

"Holly, you have to keep her safe and you

can't do that at home anymore." Colt's hand rested on her back, giving her strength.

She'd kept it together for so long. She'd managed it all without having to rely on anyone. As it came crashing down on her, she thanked God that Colt, as much as his presence troubled her, was here. Because without him, she knew she would have been alone.

"Holly, we can take her to Lakeside." Carson's gaze shifted from Colt to her and then to Opal. He smiled at her mom. "I called and they have a room available for her. She'll be less than five miles away."

"I know," Holly agreed. "I know I have to do this. I just don't know how I can." What would life be like without Opal in their home?

Colt's hand grabbed hers. "I'm here."

She nodded, unable to talk for the incredible lump in her throat.

"Carson, I have another call. If you all have this taken care of, we're going to take off." Officer Gentry spoke up. "I'm sorry about all of this, Holly. I know how tough this is for you. My grandmother has dementia."

She nodded, managing a weak attempt at a smile. "I appreciate you all bringing her here."

Dementia was the epidemic that every family understood. She only wished they didn't have to. She wished that no one ever had to suffer the loss of their memories, their loved ones, everything they'd ever known. And she wished it hadn't happened to her mother. Opal had struggled to be a good mother and just as she'd settled down, in Holly's twenties, dementia had hit, affecting her the way the drugs and mental illness had done.

"Holly, you'll probably need to drive her," Carson spoke up. "Right now she probably wouldn't get in my car."

"We can take her in my truck," Colt answered. She let him take control because she was so tired of always being the one in charge.

"I can get her clothes later." She knew her mother would be worried about that.

"But I have to go home." Opal gave her a worried look. "Where are they taking me? For surgery?"

"No, Mom, we're taking you to Lakeside Manor." Holly watched her mother's expression grow more confused and she knew there was no way to really explain. "You have friends there."

"Oh, good. I like friends."

Holly took her mother by the arm and

guided her to Colt's truck. She glanced back at the café.

"I should tell Stacy what I'm doing. They expected me to be back after dropping Dixie at school." She helped her mother into the back seat. As a precaution she flipped the child safety latch in the door.

Colt stood next to her, watching her with dark-lashed gray eyes that saw her more clearly than anyone. To everyone else, she might as well be wallpaper. She existed, but did they ever really see her?

"Call her, Holly. I'm sure everyone in that café saw what went down and they all know. Stacy is a good worker and she understands your business. Let her help." Colt opened the front passenger door. "Get in."

She stood there facing him. "You're bossy."

He grinned. She grinned. It felt good to know she could smile. She closed her eyes and thanked God, because without Him, she knew she'd be falling apart. She whispered a prayer and thanked Him for putting up with her, for understanding when she didn't go to church and for sending Colt to help her through this.

"Holly?" Colt's voice held concern.

She opened her eyes and smiled. "I'm fine.

I just needed a minute to get it together and to thank God for you. Don't let that go to your head."

"Too late." He winked and motioned her into the truck. She climbed in.

"He's a nice young man." Opal leaned forward, stretching her seat belt.

"He is," Holly agreed. "Mom, sit back so you're safe."

"I've never been a good person," Opal whispered.

"You're a good person." Holly smiled at a memory. "You built a fire once and we had s'mores for dinner. What other kid got to do that?"

"I don't know but it doesn't sound good to me," Opal said.

"It was very good."

Colt had climbed in and started the truck. "Are you ladies talking about me?"

From the back seat Opal laughed. "You're not nice. You broke Holly's heart."

"Mom!" Holly covered her face with her hands.

Colt backed the truck out of the parking space and headed for the highway. "I know I did, Opal. But I'm trying to make up for that."

"Are you going to marry her?" Opal asked.

"She won't have me." Colt glanced at Holly and she gave him the best frown she could manage. "I don't deserve her."

"That's probably true. I went for a walk earlier and I met a nice young man."

Just like that, Opal was gone. Holly knew that in time she'd disappear for good, lost inside a body with no memory of who she used to be or the people who loved her.

As they drove to Lakeside Manor, Holly let the tears slide down her cheeks unchecked. Colt dug in the console and handed her a box of tissues.

Thirty minutes later—and it didn't seem right that thirty minutes was all it took to change their lives and their family—Opal had a room at Lakeside Manor. They still had paperwork to complete and Holly would bring clothes and small personal items, but Opal was settled in room 205, a pretty yellow room with a view of the fountain.

"You can bring a bird feeder and place it outside the window," the administrator told Holly. "Our residents find peace in watching the birds."

Opal walked to the window. "Is that pond for me?"

"The fountain, Opal. And yes. Later today

we will take a walk out there, when it's a bit warmer. We'll also make a necklace during craft time." The administrator smiled at Holly. "There are no set visiting hours so you stay as long as you'd like. You can visit at any time and you can even take meals with your mother."

"Thank you." Holly joined her mother at the window. "Mom, I know this is difficult."

"What is?" Opal asked, unsure. "I like to visit. As soon as lunch is over, we can go home."

"Mom, I can't take you home." The words came out on a sob.

"Of course you can," Opal argued. "You brought me here."

"I know." Holly reached for her mother's hand and held it tight. "I'm sorry. I hope you'll forgive me."

Opal didn't respond. Her gaze remained fixed on the fountain.

"Mom, you have to stay here. When I leave, you'll stay. This is your new home. But we'll visit. Dixie and I will visit you. We'll make s'mores and have them for dinner."

"That's very bad for you," Opal told her. "You should eat more, Holly. You've lost weight and you look tired."

"I am tired, Mom."

"You should get some rest." Opal turned from the window and looked at her. "I'm sorry for calling the police."

"You didn't..." She shook her head. It would do no good to remind Opal of what had happened. "I'm going home now to get your clothes."

"Okay. Make sure you come back to get me. I know I have a home. I don't think I want to stay here."

Holly hugged her mother.

"It'll be okay," Opal said. "Dixie is here now. You take care of her."

"I will." Holly made her way to the door where Colt waited for her.

She allowed him to pull her into her arms, even as she told herself she shouldn't get used to it, to him being there for her. Yes, he had proposed but that had been his way of handling their shared custody of Dixie and not the kind of proposal a woman dreams about.

Every woman dreamed of forever with a man who loved and cherished her. Colt was good at making her feel cherished, but love was about more than feelings. It was a commitment.

Colt wasn't good at commitment.

Chapter Eight

By Friday, Holly and Dixie had settled into a routine. Colt helped out by picking Dixie up from school and bringing her to the café. They were building their relationships, becoming a family. But to Holly, they weren't a family. Colt still planned on returning to bullfighting, and Dixie missed Daisy and her life in Broken Arrow. Holly understood. Their daughter had lost the woman who had been her mother. She'd been taken from her home, away from everything familiar.

If she still seemed a little lost, that was only natural.

Holly had been doing research, trying to find the best way to help Dixie deal with her grief.

As she navigated the tables of the café, her

mind focused on her daughter, she tripped over her own feet. The tray she carried tilted and the glasses and water pitcher tilted and slid forward. A hand shot out to steady her, but it was too late for the contents of her tray.

"Let me help you." Colt released her arm and took the tray that she hadn't dropped, setting it on a nearby table. The few customers who were in the café for coffee and late breakfast watched as Colt grabbed a towel. If the heat in her cheeks was anything to go by, her face was most likely turning a brilliant shade of crimson.

"This is embarrassing," she murmured as she bent down to pick up the plastic glasses. Colt reached for a couple that had rolled away.

Her right-hand woman, Stacy, arrived with towels and a mop.

"Boss, let me deal with this. Why don't you get a cup of coffee and something to eat?" Stacy gave her a steady, concerned look.

"I'm really okay," Holly assured her employee.

"Uh-huh," Stacy murmured with a doubtful look.

"What?" Holly asked as she sopped up nearly a gallon of water with the towels the other woman had arrived with.

"Nothing," Stacy said as she mopped up the remaining spill. "I'm not saying anything."

"Well, I'm saying something." Colt knelt next to her and took the sopping wet towels.

Holly's chest felt tight and she closed her eyes against the wave of emotion, of feeling lost, feeling...she squeezed her eyes tighter. She didn't want to feel as if he was there to take care of her. She took care of herself. Always. That's what she had to remember.

She opened her eyes and pushed to her feet, and he followed. They stood there in a silent stare down with witnesses.

The last thing she wanted to be was the afternoon gossip. She'd been that often enough in her life. This is why she lived a quiet life, the kind of life that didn't give rise to speculation or rumor.

Colt's expression turned tender as he gazed at her. He had wet towels in his hands. It was her perfect opportunity to walk away. But Stacy had finished mopping and she took the towels from him and handed him a dry towel for his hands. He used it, then took her by the arm and led her to the empty back dining room.

"Colt, too bad you didn't have the same

charm with that bull that got you down," Chet yelled from across the café.

Colt stopped at the door to respond.

"Chet, if I had charmed that bull, I would have ruined him for his owner. He would have walked out of that arena and never bucked again."

A lot of laughter followed the statement.

"You're so sure of yourself," Holly said as he sat down across from her. "Are you comparing me to a bull?"

"You are definitely not a bull," he answered. "And Chet expects that kind of response."

That made her wonder if she really knew him. Was he being who *she* wanted him to be, rather than who he really was?

"Stacy, can you get us an omelet?" Colt called out to the waitress as she walked out of the kitchen. "And hash browns."

"Sure thing," Stacy did a one-eighty and headed back into the kitchen.

"Are you ordering food for me?" Holly asked him.

He tipped his hat back, giving her a better view of gray eyes that danced with mirth. "Yep."

She didn't argue. It would be pointless, and

now that she'd sat down for a minute, she realized she was hungry. She knew she needed to eat more. Her clothes were baggy, her face hollow. Every time Colt looked at her, she wondered if he saw the old Holly or the real woman sitting before him now.

"Holly, when was the last time you ate?"

It wasn't a question she wanted to answer. She'd had dinner the previous evening and then she'd helped Dixie with homework before their nightly visit to Opal. This morning she'd gotten the café going, gone home to get Dixie ready for school and then stopped by to see Opal before heading back to work.

Colt removed his hat, ran a hand through his hair and replaced the hat. "From your silence I'm assuming you haven't eaten today. You've got to take care of yourself. Not just for Dixie and Opal, but for you. I won't always be here to make sure you eat."

"I know that. And I do eat."

"I worry about you." He said it tenderly and she felt tears close to falling. She blinked them away but she couldn't undo the way his words touched her.

She wanted to sleep. She wanted to take time to get a pedicure or get her hair done.

Stacy arrived with the omelet, hash browns,

biscuits and gravy. The plate was overflowing with food. "There you go, Hol, make sure you eat it all."

"Bring him a plate. He's going to have to help." Holly smiled up at her waitress,

"You got it."

"I had breakfast," he informed her.

"You can eat more. You could always eat," she said. The man she used to know could. She wasn't completely sure about this man.

Holly was finishing the omelet when Colt's phone rang. He answered it, looked concerned, then got up and limped away from the table, rubbing the back of his neck as he stood a short distance away. Holly watched as he glanced back at her, as if she was a subject of the call.

Minutes later he returned, worry lines appearing across his forehead. "Dixie isn't at school. They said she was there for her morning classes and then they went to the library and now she's missing."

Holly pushed the chair back from the table and stood. "Let's go."

Holly headed for the kitchen. Stacy was going to need a raise, she thought as she hurried to find her waitress. And a promotion.

Stacy was washing a few dishes but she stopped when she saw Holly. "What's up?"

"I have to go. The school called and Dixie isn't there."

"Of course you should go," Stacy said, giving her a quick hug. "I know you'll find her. Maybe she just needed some space."

"Thank you." Holly hugged the woman back. "I owe you a raise and a promotion."

"Go on, we'll be just fine here." Stacy gave her a little push toward the door. "Jess Larson wants a job. If I get busy, I'll call her in."

"It's only a few blocks to the school. Do we drive or walk?" Colt asked as they left the café.

"I think walk." She gave him a careful look as he limped along next to her. "Will you be okay?"

He pounded his chest with a fist. "You wound me. Of course I'm fine. Each day gets a little better. So did Dixie seem off to you this morning? Did anything seem different?"

"Not really," Holly said, slowing her pace as they turned onto the street that led to the school. "Of course she's still sad. She misses her mom, her life. And Daisy. Do you think she's run away, back to Broken Arrow?"

It hurt to think about, but it was a reality

they had to face. Daisy had been a large part of Dixie's life. In less than two months, they would sit down with a lawyer and decide final custody arrangements, and Dixie might very well choose Colt's sister. Then what? Holly didn't want to think about Dixie not being in her home or part her life. And Colt? No doubt he'd hook his camper to his truck and go back to work, traveling from rodeo to rodeo.

And Holly would be left alone.

She pushed the thoughts aside because right now she had to focus on today, on Dixie. She thought about that verse from Matthew, that today's troubles are enough in themselves. No need to worry about tomorrow and something she couldn't fix or change.

"I know she loves my sister, but Daisy is young and unsettled. She's wild as a firecracker, as my dad liked to say."

Colt reached for her hand. They walked past the park pavilion and he pulled her into the shade of the domed shelter.

"We have to keep looking," she told him.

"You have to be calm so that when we find her, you'll be reasonable." He pulled a handkerchief out of his pocket and started to dab at her cheeks.

"Is that thing clean?" she asked as she

grabbed it out of his hand, stopping him from wiping her face.

"Of course it is. I carry two. One for myself and one for damsels."

"I'm a damsel, am I?"

"In need of rescuing," he told her as he pushed a strand of hair behind her ear. "Wipe your eyes."

She did, then she folded the handkerchief and slid it into the front pocket of her jeans. "I'm calm."

"As much as can be expected. We should keep looking."

He leaned in, his cheek close to hers. She thought he was going to kiss her, which made no sense. But then he took her by the shoulders and turned her around.

"She's right over there," he pointed.

Looking in that direction, she saw her daughter sitting under an oak tree, a big black dog curled up next to her. "Where did she find a dog?"

"I don't know." He took hold of her arm. "Let's go get our daughter."

Colt let her lead the way as they crossed the expanse of park. As they walked, she noticed the grass coming up was as green as emeralds. A perfect spring day, full of hope. But their daughter, curled up next to a stray dog, tears streaming down her cheeks, didn't seem to feel that hope.

Dixie didn't look up. She had her arms around the dog, and the dog shot them a warning look. Holly sank to the ground, sitting close to Dixie, pulling her into her arms and holding her tight.

"I miss my mom." Dixie sobbed into Holly's shoulder. "I try not to cry but I can't help it. And I didn't want to cry in school and have everyone see."

Holly brushed Dixie's hair back from her face. "You don't have to hide your tears or the fact that you're sad. You have every right to cry and to grieve your mom."

"Dixie, promise us next time, you'll go to someone in the school and tell them you need us," Colt said as he leaned against the tree, his hand on their daughter's head. "You don't have to be alone. You have us. We're all new at this, but we're a family."

Colt slid down to sit on the other side of Dixie and the dog. The three of them sat together under the tree. Struggling to find their way.

They were doing better than Holly thought. Dixie sharing with them, holding on to them, surely that meant they were becoming more than strangers trying to be a family?

Colt ran his hand over the head of the big dog that studied them but remained close to Dixie. He didn't know what else to say to their daughter. He could make promises that things would get easier. He could promise her ponies. But even he knew that words and promises weren't going to take her away pain. Time. Love. Understanding. Those were the things she needed.

"We were worried," Holly said.

"I'm sorry. I just…" She shrugged. "I don't know. It's just that I feel like I don't belong anywhere. I'm here but I don't know if this is my home. I guess I wonder why you would want me now when you didn't want me before."

Her words struck hard. From the look on Holly's face, she felt it, too. Neither of them had considered the pain and worry that Dixie had been feeling. They were all about her grief, but man, to be here with the two people who had given her up for adoption, thinking they hadn't ever wanted her…

"You are wanted," Colt said, not knowing

exactly how to make her believe those words. "You are *very* wanted."

"But you gave me away," she countered. Her hand dashed away more tears.

"We weren't very grown-up at the time," Holly told her. "We wanted you. I promise you we did. I..."

He knew what Holly had wanted. She'd wanted them to be a family. But he'd been too selfish at the time to give her what she wanted.

"We wanted you to have more than we could give you," he finished for Holly.

Holly drew in a breath and Dixie half climbed into her lap.

"Dixie, we wanted you then and we want you now." Holly spoke gently, her cheek resting on Dixie's head.

"I know," Dixie mumbled against Holly's shoulder, the dog moving in closer. "I just miss...everything."

"What do you miss?" Holly asked. "Is there something we can do to make you more comfortable?"

"I miss my old life. I miss my mom, my friends, my house, my stuffed animals." She sniffled and sat back up, pulling the dog close again. "I miss Daisy. We used to go get pedicures."

"We need to do more fun stuff," Holly said, her face pale. "I don't know why I didn't think about that. We should do more fun things together."

"It's okay," Dixie told her. "You'll figure it out."

"Where are your stuffed animals? The rest of your stuff?" Colt asked. He hadn't even thought about that when he picked her up in Broken Arrow. She was eleven. She had things that she cared about, things that made her feel safe. Where were those things? He should have asked Daisy.

"I don't know," she whispered. "I think most of it is at Daisy's."

"I'll find out and we'll go get it."

"We can?" She brightened up. "I have a blanket with pandas and I have a sloth stuffed animal. He's my favorite. And all my books."

All of her life packed up in boxes and taken where? She'd lost her mom. She shouldn't have to lose everything that meant something to her.

Holly looked up, her brown eyes seeking reassurance from him, asking him to make this better for their daughter. He gave a quick nod. He would make sure. He only hoped this wasn't going to be a promise he broke.

"Where'd you get this dog?" Holly asked as she stood, pulling Dixie to her feet with her. The dog also stood, slowly, stretching as he did. He was a huge animal, with a black shaggy coat and dark eyes that studied them as if he might have to hurt them if they weren't careful with his new best friend.

"He was at the church and when he saw me, he came over to hang out with me." Dixie hugged the dog. "Do you think he belongs to someone?"

"I'm sure he must. He looks well taken care of," Holly gave the dog a pat. "We should try to find his owners."

"Oh." Dixie looked heartbroken.

"Let's head over to the church to see what's going on. Maybe they know whose dog it is." Colt started to push himself to his feet and Holly reached over, giving him a hand.

"Come on, old guy, let me help you up," she teased.

Dixie laughed so he decided he wouldn't argue too much. He took Holly's hand and she pulled him to his feet. He didn't immediately let go of her hand. Instead he pulled her close and kissed her cheek.

"Gross. I told you, no PDA." Dixie shook her head, then she said to the dog, "That's what happens when grown-ups fall in love. I'm never going to have a boyfriend. They're gross."

Colt ruffled her hair, messing it up and making her groan and brush it down again.

This was what it felt like to be a family. Even with the grief, the hard times, the worry, it felt good. This was what it was like to have Holly at his side, her fingers brushing his, interlocking briefly before sliding away again.

Today he could almost believe that this was their future, the three of them as a family.

When they got to the church he realized he should have recognized the car and the trucks. His brother and Kylie were outside the church looking at windows. Pastor Stevens stood next to them. Jack sat on a nearby bench with Maria at his side.

"Cooter, there you are. I wondered where you'd gotten off to." Kylie greeted the dog. Cooter nudged at Dixie as if giving her a goodbye hug and then he settled in next to Kylie.

"What are the three of you doing out and about?" Carson asked, glancing at his watch and ignoring—in his big brother way—the fact that it was a school day.

"Taking a walk," Colt answered.

"Cooter came over to say hi to me," Dixie said. There was a telltale hiccup in her voice and noticeable puffiness around her eyes.

Kylie studied her for a moment. Then she said, "Cooter likes to hang out with us. When we come to the church, he usually heads for the park to see if there is anyone around to play with. I usually don't worry because he's friendly and he always comes back. But he seems to really like you."

"I like him, too." Dixie petted the dog's head and Cooter closed his eyes as if he'd found the best kid in the world. "What kind of dog is he?"

"He's a labradoodle," Kylie answered, looking from the dog to Colt's daughter. "He's pretty special. He likes to help people feel better."

Colt watched in wonder as his daughter practically lit up, petting the dog who seemed to understand that she needed him. He moved closer to her side, and it made sense, that Cooter had found her at the park and curled up next to her under that tree.

Dixie needed a dog. He glanced at Holly,

wondering if she thought the same. Would she agree to letting their daughter have a dog like Cooter, one trained to make her feel secure in her new environment? He thought it could help. The old beagle he'd had as a kid had been his best friend when things had gone south with his parents. When they'd fight, he'd go find old Snoop and spend time in the barn with the tricolored animal with the small body, long ears and big heart.

"We should be going," Holly said. "Someone has had a break from school but probably needs to return. Although…we might be able to get lunch first."

Dixie's smile disappeared at the mention of school. "Can we eat at the café?" she asked.

"Of course," Holly responded. "I need to get back to work so we can have lunch while we're there."

"Maybe I could stay with you today and help?"

Colt guessed Holly was going to object but she just nodded. "Yes, I think that's a good idea. I'll call the school and let them know. I'll also call and make an appointment with Rebecca West for pedicures."

"We can do pedicures?" Dixie asked.

"At Rebecca's Salon. It's right across the

street from the café. Remember, she's Isaac's wife."

"I remember. And Allie's mom," Dixie said. She lit up a little, the sadness momentarily chased away. She hugged Holly and then leaned down to hug the dog, Cooter.

"Holly, could we talk for a minute?" Kylie asked, her knowing gaze on Cooter and Dixie.

"Of course," Holly answered.

"Dixie, can you keep an eye on Cooter for me?" Kylie asked. "Don't let him wander off."

Dixie nodded and she was already on the ground with the dog. Colt watched her for a moment and then his gaze followed Holly as she walked away with Kylie. He hoped the outcome of this conversation was another new addition to the family.

He watched Kylie and Holly talk, their heads close together in conversation, and he found himself praying, for all of them. They had a tough road ahead, tougher than he would have imagined.

Looking back he guessed he'd rushed in on his proverbial white horse, thinking he'd rescue Dixie, make Holly grateful, and the three of them would have a happily-ever-after.

Reality was never quite as easy as all that.

Chapter Nine

❧

"Would you do me a favor?" Kylie asked.

Holly studied her friend's face, wondering at the slightly sneaky expression. "What are you up to?"

Kylie grinned at the question. "I want you to adopt Cooter. He's a sweet dog. I've been training him for a year and he's somewhat silly, but he's housebroken and sensitive."

Kylie, in addition to being a therapist, raised service animals. They were well-trained animals taught to comfort, to recognize different situations in their owners' lives, and some were guide dogs for those with physical challenges. Holly should have recognized Cooter as one of Kylie's animals.

Colt's niece Allie suffered from seizures, and she had a special dog that had been trained to sense when a seizure was coming on and to protect her if she fell during a seizure.

"Didn't you have him for someone?"

"Not really. Jack was going to take him but now he worries about the dog not getting enough exercise. I think he also worried that he might trip over an animal."

"Dixie needs him." Holly glanced back at her daughter and the sweet dog that had remained close by her side. "Is that what you're saying?"

"Maybe he needs her," Kylie offered. "And if school was tough for her today, maybe give her a day or two with you. Call the school counselor and let them know that she's struggling, that you can do schoolwork at home and she'll be seeing me. If you want her to see me."

"I do think she needs to talk to someone," Holly agreed. "If you have the time, we'll make an appointment."

"I always have time for Dixie." Kylie paused. "And for you and Colt if needed. This has been a huge change for all three of you."

"It has, but we're working through it." Holly glanced back at her daughter.

"Is there something more, Holly? None of us know the entire situation with Dixie's custody."

"She's only here with us for two months, then she'll choose where she wants to go. That was the way Becky's will laid out the question of guardianship."

Kylie cringed. "Wow, that's tough. I'm not sure that's in Dixie's best interest. Her having to choose is going to put a lot of stress on her."

"I agree, but what can we do? Some days it feels like Daisy and I will be the two women going before King Solomon, both claiming that the baby is ours. I won't tear her apart and make her choose. If it comes down to it, I'll give custody to Daisy."

"What if that isn't what Dixie wants?"

"I don't know, Kylie. I know that it isn't fair to Dixie to have to make this choice. But it also isn't fair that she's been taken from everything familiar just weeks after losing her mother. I'm basically a stranger to her."

"I know." Kylie gave her a quick hug. "With that all in mind, let's start having weekly talks. I'll come over to the house to talk to Dixie, so she feels comfortable."

"Thank you."

Kylie nodded in the direction of Dixie and

Colt. "Why don't you tell your daughter she has a dog? I'll stop by with a bag of his favorite food and bring his collar and service animal vest."

They headed back to Colt and Dixie. At the sight of Kylie, Cooter cocked his head to the side, his ears perking up.

"Can we go now?" Dixie asked, a big grin on her face. "We have a surprise."

"What a coincidence, because so do I." Holly hugged her daughter. "You go first."

"No, you go first!" Dixie told her. "What is it?"

"Cooter's going to come live with us."

"What about the cats?" Dixie questioned. "That might be trouble."

Kylie laughed. "Cooter loves cats."

Holly looked to Colt and saw approval. He grinned, those gray eyes of his twinkling with amusement. And something else. Something just for her. It made her feel nineteen again. Nineteen and in love.

But she wasn't in love. She knew that he was gorgeous, and attraction wasn't love.

Dixie hugged Kylie, then turned to Holly. "Now our surprise."

"What's your surprise?" Holly asked.

"D..." Dixie stopped herself. She looked

from Holly to Colt and took a deep breath. "Dad made us an appointment at the salon to get a pedicure. He's taking us right now."

"But I have to work," Holly blurted out, which she quickly regretted because Dixie's happy expression crumpled and Kylie shook her head. "But…work can wait."

The café would still be there, and she had employees who could take care of the business in her absence. But Dixie might not always be here.

They said their goodbyes to Kylie and Carson, as well as Pastor Stevens, and headed back toward the café. Dixie walked ahead of them, Cooter on a leash next to her. Colt reached for Holly's hand and she laced her fingers through his because it felt right.

"Thank you," she told him.

"For what?"

"Thinking of us, making the appointment at the salon, being here. It's a long list."

"I wouldn't be anywhere else."

She gave him a long look. "Really?"

"Really. I know that's hard for you to believe, but this is where I want to be. I want to be with you and Dixie."

"What if she chooses Daisy?" Holly whispered the question, making sure Dixie didn't hear. Saying the words out loud made them real, and it hurt.

"I'm trying not to think about that."

"Me, either," she said. "I don't want to think about how empty my house and my life will be. And then I tell myself how selfish that is."

"It isn't selfish."

"Kind of is," she said as he pulled her closer to his side. "Kylie is going to meet with Dixie. She doesn't agree with the will, with putting so much pressure on Dixie to make the decision about guardianship. I understand that Becky wanted her to have a say, but it's a lot for a young girl to handle."

"I couldn't agree more. As happy as I was to know we could bring her here and spend time together, I worried about how it will affect her later on."

"Then knowing that, we have to be the ones who help her make a decision that won't hurt. As much." Even if it hurt them.

"Deal."

Holly didn't say it out loud, but they were thinking the same thing. Dixie's life was back in Broken Arrow, with Daisy. In Broken Arrow there were friends, dance lessons, soccer and all of the other things that were familiar and beloved.

They could visit her there. The drive was easy; less than two hours They could stay in her life. But if she made the choice to go back, it would hurt. She would be gone from Hope. Colt would go back on the road. Holly would go back to burying herself in work.

Today, though, they had one another. They made their way up the sidewalk to Rebecca's Lakeside Drive Salon and Day Spa where Colt had arranged for them both to have pedicures and shoulder massages.

They entered the salon, which was across the street from Holly's café. Rebecca called out a greeting from the back where she was doing a perm.

"My nail girl will be right with you and I'll join her as soon as I finish up here." Rebecca said as she moved her client to the hair dryer.

Holly led Dixie to the pedicure chairs with the massaging seats.

"You girls have fun," Colt told them as they got settled.

Dixie had to scoot down in the seat so her feet could reach the basin for the water, even though it hadn't been filled yet.

"Where are you going?" Holly asked.

He grinned and started backing toward the door. "I have a café to run. You're fired."

"What? You can't fire me. I own that café."

"I own 51 percent if I remember correctly. I've been an amazing silent partner for a few years but I realize I've overlooked my duties. Don't consider this a permanent firing. But for the next six weeks, you're laid off."

"Colt, you don't know the first thing about running the café. You can't cook. You can't wait tables."

Dixie began to laugh. "Oh, yeah, that's the other surprise. He *can* cook. And he's really firing you."

"Not funny." She started to get out of the chair but Dixie shook her head. "I can't let him do this. He'll ruin my business."

"I think he's serious," Dixie said with a bit of a smirk.

Holly settled back into her seat, Dixie's words taking the wind from her sails. Colt stood at the door, his expression serious, but ultimately he would let her make the final decision.

Finally, she nodded. "I think I just lost my job."

Dixie clapped her hands. "Pedicure time."

Colt waved goodbye. Holly wanted it to

be this way forever, them spending time together, making decisions together, but she knew time was short, and eventually a decision needed to be made.

And she didn't get to choose.

Colt walked out the door of the salon feeling pretty pleased with himself, yet also scared to death. That was hard to admit. He hadn't planned it this way. He thought he'd help more, take on more responsibility. But laying Holly off from her own diner had been a whim. He'd had the advantage of shocking her.

He grinned and began to whistle as he crossed the street. As he headed up the sidewalk to the café, Isaac parked and got out of his truck.

"Someone looks happy," Isaac said as he joined him. "Did you get her to say yes?"

"Nope." Colt opened the door of the café and motioned his brother inside. Isaac was his brother. That was still a hard thing to accept, even after all these years. Sometimes he thought they didn't know each other any better than he and Dixie did.

Or Holly. He had known the little girl Holly. He'd met up with her at that college in

Tulsa. But really knowing her? That was just now starting to happen.

He guessed a guy should truly know a woman before he proposed spending the rest of his life with her.

"So why are you whistling?" Isaac followed him through the café, calling out a few greetings as he dogged Colt's steps to the kitchen. "You're back to your happy face. She didn't say yes. But you're happy. And you were at the salon."

"I made her a pedicure appointment. Holly and Dixie are doing what girls do."

"Good job," Isaac complimented. "And *that's* why you're whistling?"

Colt walked into the kitchen, where Stacy and Jess, the waitress in training, turned to give him confused and questioning looks.

"Everything okay?" Stacy asked.

He looked around the kitchen and the café, his new domain. "I fired Holly."

"You did *what*?" Big ol' Jim, the best fry cook in the county, came around the counter toward him.

Isaac laughed but Colt didn't see this as a laughing matter. Jim happened to be a pretty big guy, and he was loyal to Holly.

Colt held up a hand to stop the beating he

was about to get from a man who didn't look too amused by his choice of words.

"Temporarily," he rushed to explain. "She needs to rest and spend time with her daughter. As her silent partner in this business, I've decided to speak up. In the best interest of the café, and in Holly and Dixie's best interest, I'm taking over for a few weeks."

Isaac sat down on a stool, hand to his left ear. "Could you repeat that, because I'm sure I didn't catch everything you said."

"You heard me." Colt turned to his half brother. "Now get out of my kitchen. I have work to do."

"Nah, I think I'll stick around. Watching you be the chief cook and bottle washer might be good entertainment." Isaac grew serious. "Also, I have a message and a gift to deliver."

"What would that be?" Colt asked as he glanced around the kitchen, wondering what the owner of a café was supposed to do.

"Dad wants to give his granddaughter a gift. I'm supposed to deliver it this evening."

"What kind of gift?" Colt asked as he stuck his head out the door and surveyed the dining area, where Stacy was filling drinks and taking orders.

The door to the kitchen flew open and

Stacy rushed in with a tray, an order pad and a pitcher of water. "Get to work. *Boss*."

She tossed him the order pad and shoved him toward the door. "The lunch crowd has arrived."

He stepped into the dining room and thought maybe he'd made a mistake about this new career path. Ten tables of happy, joking citizens of Hope. They were all laughing; many were looking at their phones. And then they were looking at him.

Colt smiled at the crowd and turned back to the kitchen. Smile gone, he walked up to Isaac and pushed him off the stool, laughing as Isaac tried to keep his feet under him. Isaac's phone slipped from his hand and Colt hurried to grab it while Isaac scrambled to keep it from him. Colt got to it first.

He went straight to texts and saw what he guessed he would see. One text to dozens of people. Colt has a new job as a waitress at Holly's.

"Nice," Colt told his brother. "That's your way of helping me?"

"I thought Holly could use the business. It's called marketing, brother."

"You thought you wanted a job washing dishes, that's what you thought." Colt grabbed an apron and a pair of rubber gloves, and pushed them into Isaac's unwilling hands. "Have fun."

Isaac's laughter chased Colt from the room. He might not have experience but he was quick on his feet. Well, not quick. He had a leg that knotted up and a back that had seen better days, but he could peddle a fried chicken special and pour sweet tea.

Each time he entered the kitchen, he saw Isaac elbow-deep in suds, washing the dishes that either Colt or Stacy brought in by the tub load.

At one point Isaac stretched and pushed his hands against his lower back. "I know what I'm getting Holly for Christmas."

"What's that?" Isaac asked.

"A dishwasher, the automatic kind that doesn't require a man to be on his feet for hours. Is this rush about over with?"

"I think it is. In fifteen minutes you can have a break. Remember, marketing, brother."

Isaac grabbed the sprayer from the sink and turned to aim it at Colt.

"Don't do it," Colt told him.

"Do you understand I have work to do? I have a job running a ranch. And I'm supposed to be loading up a horse for your daughter."

"That's all pretty nice and I'm glad to hear about the job. Most of us didn't think you'd amount to much."

"That's low." Isaac hit the water and sprayed Colt in the face.

Seconds later the two of them were fighting over the hose, spraying water as they wrestled each other for possession. Sputtering and laughing, they backed away from each other, taking the towels that Jess offered as she ventured back into the kitchen.

"That was uncalled for." Isaac wiped his face with a towel and tossed it to Colt. "Uh-oh…"

Colt wiped water from his face and pushed his hair back out of his eyes. And there was Holly standing in front of him, hands on her hips. He glanced down and saw that her toenails were a pretty shade of pink.

"Nice color," he stated before she whacked him with a towel.

"I've worked hard to build up this business. The two of you are *not* going to destroy it in a day. You're both fired."

"Sorry," Colt grinned. "But I'm staying. And you're going. We've got this under control."

"I. Don't. Work. For. You," Isaac stated, as

he ran his fingers through his hair. "I can't stay here washing your dishes. I have a job. Hire a dishwasher." Isaac pulled a wallet from his back pocket. "I'll write you a check right now to buy a dishwasher for this place."

"That's a waste of money," Holly informed him. "I wash dishes when I get a break from working out front. It saves money."

Isaac wrote out a check and handed it to her. "Consider it a wedding gift."

She gave him a look that sent him running for the door.

"Isaac, I have the right to refuse service to anyone," she warned.

"I'm sorry, Holly. It was a joke, really. I wouldn't wish anyone tied down to him. He'd be rotten as a husband."

Colt wanted her to disagree, but she didn't. Instead she pointed to the door and Isaac went.

"You have to dry the floor before someone slips and gets hurt," Holly told Colt. Standing in front of him, her arms were crossed.

He started to say something to Jim but realized the other man had disappeared. Smart. Colt started thinking maybe he should have escaped as well. But then, if he had, he wouldn't be in here alone with Holly.

Then he noticed something. "You got your hair done," he said.

She touched the soft strands, and he was suddenly jealous that he wasn't smoothing his fingers through her hair. The style wasn't much of a change, just a trim that left it looking softer around her face.

"Rebecca said you gave her too much money, so she insisted I get my hair styled."

"I'm glad she did." He took a step closer. "I'm sorry about the floor. Me and Isaac got a little out of control."

"I can see that."

"How was the mother-daughter bonding time?"

She smiled, and the expression undid something inside him. That look made him want to send her to the salon every day of the week.

"It was perfect. Thank you for that. I should have thought of it. I just… I don't know, I thought having her here was enough."

"You are enough, Holly. She just needed some special time alone with you. I'd like to have some time alone with you, too. Dinner, maybe a movie?"

She shook her head. "This isn't about us, Colt. It's about Dixie."

He disagreed but didn't say so.

Instead he reached up, smoothing the soft fall of bangs that swept across her brow. She closed her eyes as he pushed the hair back from her face.

Slowly he leaned in and kissed her cheek. She opened her eyes, a fleeting smile softening her lips and then disappearing.

"That was nice," she said. "But I don't think you're supposed to kiss customers. I'm here for lunch."

"I'm the boss, I make the rules," he informed her.

"Maybe so, but I have my own rules. We'd like two burgers and two orders of fries to go. And make it snappy." She laughed as she stood on tiptoe and kissed him, quick and easy, as if they did this every day.

"For you, anything at all."

"You can join us, if you like," she suggested.

First he had the clean up the floor. "Could you send Jim back here? I think we scared him off."

Holly laughed as she headed out of the kitchen. "I guess since I'm fired, you'll have to find Jim for yourself and convince him not to hurt you."

That went better than expected. Maybe,

just maybe, they had a chance at being a real family and not just two strangers sharing a child.

Colt had always been an optimist at heart.

Chapter Ten

Holly spent Saturday with Dixie. The two of them worked on clearing out the garden at the house, preparing it for spring flowers. Later in the afternoon, they visited Opal. It ached every time she had to tell her mother she couldn't go home, knowing that Opal didn't fully understand. In her lucid moments she was very capable of being at home and she knew it. But those days were growing fewer and fewer.

On their way home, she and Dixie both shed a few tears over the goodbye with Opal, when she'd pleaded to go home until an aide had redirected her to the game room.

As they pulled up the driveway, Holly saw that Cooter had been turned loose and Colt's truck was parked near the barn. Colt was nowhere in sight, but Cooter saw them and hurried to greet them as they got out of the car.

"Where's Colt?" Dixie asked as she scanned the yard.

"Your guess is as good as mine." She didn't see him, but she smelled something mouth-watering.

"What is that?" Dixie asked. "I wasn't hungry until now."

"I'm not sure but I'm guessing if we head for the back patio, we'll find out."

"I hope it tastes as good as it smells," Dixie said as she hurried ahead. Cooter ran alongside her, licking at her hands as they ran. Holly didn't have the energy for running. She was feeling better since Colt's forced vacation, and she could tell that he'd been right. She wasn't as healthy as she should be. Working full time and caring for Opal had taken a toll on her that she'd tried to deny.

She should have taken better care of herself. She should have taken days off.

Shoulda. Woulda. Coulda.

Instead of walking to the patio, Dixie headed toward the big oak tree at the side of the house, Holly following close behind. They spied a saucer-shaped swing hanging from the tree. Dixie didn't waste time climbing on.

"Watch how high I go!" Dixie yelled.

"I am!" Holly called back.

She walked toward the back patio, a square of broken concrete that needed repairs. Like everything around here, the patio had been neglected. The table was from the last century, literally. The chairs had been repaired too many times to count, and there was a crack in the glass tabletop. And she'd failed to water her plants. Again.

Colt came out the back door carrying a spatula, wearing a red apron. He looked silly standing there in jeans, T-shirt, cowboy hat and boots with that red apron hanging almost to his knees. Silly but so attractive her knees felt weak. She shook off whatever feelings were stirring in her heart and refocused on the planters next to the patio, the ones she hadn't gotten to that day. From the looks of them, she hadn't gotten to them in a lot of days.

"Why the long face?" Colt asked.

"No reason," she fibbed. "What are you making?"

Colt lifted the grill lid. "Tri-tip. Smoked to perfection."

"It smells amazing."

"It'll taste amazing, too," he told her as he

closed the lid. "And you're not being honest with me. Why are you giving the plants a dirty look?"

Holly let her gaze slide back to the wilted and dying plants in the earthen containers at the edge of the patio.

"As far as I can tell, they aren't much to look at. In fact, calling them plants might be an overstatement." He grinned, and she found the humor in the situation. Barely.

"Well, they started out as plants. And I took care of them for a while. And then I got busy, and I found I just didn't care about them enough. Each day I walked past them and saw that they needed water. And I always thought, 'Tomorrow. I'll take care of them tomorrow.'"

He nodded, his smile disappearing. "Go on."

"I put everything off until tomorrow. What if I do that to Dixie? What if I keep thinking, 'Tomorrow,' and then I fail to be a mom because I get too busy?"

"You're overthinking this, Hol. Just be her mom. Today you were her mom and you did an excellent job."

"You think I did, but what if I forget to feed her?"

He laughed at that. "You've met her. Do

you think she's going to let you go more than a couple of hours without feeding her?"

She watched their daughter swinging, Cooter running back and forth next to her. Laughter rang out as the dog tried to get on the swing with Dixie. She was being a normal little girl of eleven. For the moment everything was good.

"Stop overthinking," Colt told her as he lifted the grill lid to check the progress of their dinner.

Holly leaned in next to him, inhaling the aroma. "That smells so good."

"I told you I could cook," he said, turning the grill to Low, then taking a seat at the table. She sat next to him, both of them watching Dixie on the swing.

"You did, but I had to see it to believe it."

His face fell. "I want you to believe in a lot more than my ability to cook."

"I do believe in more than your ability to cook," she told him. "Why is your truck parked by the barn? Because I also believe that the swing and grill are not the only new things on my property."

He laughed. "I was working on the fence and putting a few things in the tack room."

"What kind of things?"

"Probably tack," he countered as he got himself to his feet and returned to the grill.

"Tack for what?" she asked. He gave her a little grin.

"Grandpa Jack has a gift for Dixie."

"A gift?" she asked. But she thought she knew what it was, and her heart took flight at the kindness the Wests were showing Dixie.

Colt glanced at his watch and then he winked. "I would say to count to about a hundred and she'll scream like a banshee."

She didn't have to count. A minute later a truck and trailer came up the drive, pulling past the house to the barn. A horse whinnied from inside the trailer. Colt had been right. Dixie let out a squeal and ran in the direction of the trailer. Colt caught her as she ran past him.

"Slow down and let him park. You don't want to be behind the trailer if he has to back up."

"There are two horses in there!" Dixie yelled. "TWO!"

"Two?" Holly walked next to him. "Why two?"

"Because Jack thought both of our girls need pretty ponies. Not that these are ponies." Colt kept walking as he imparted that bit of information, Dixie glued close to his side, bouncing as she walked.

To Holly it seemed like a lot, those two horses. She couldn't even keep plants alive. Worse, she pictured herself here, alone, two horses grazing in the field, reminding her of what she had and lost.

But she couldn't let herself worry about the future of their situation. Best to just focus on what was happening at the moment. It was a hard lesson to learn, to put aside her worries, to focus on the here and now, to breathe and enjoy the journey. Why did it come so much easier to some people? She envied those people. She wanted to be more like them.

She stepped close to Colt, who was standing to the side, waiting for Isaac to back the trailer near the corral.

He grabbed her around the waist and gathered both her and Dixie close.

Dixie stopped bouncing and started wringing her hands. Holly smiled at her daughter. Retraining her worrisome brain would take time but Holly found she wanted to let go of the worries. They weighed a lot, all of those troubling thoughts did.

She wanted to be more like the girl she used to be, the one who knew her family was a little messed up but she wore the unicorn costume, ran barefoot all summer, swam in the creek with her best friend and laughed often.

"Can I call Daisy?" Dixie had gone still and didn't look at them, instead keeping her gaze on the horse trailer.

"Of course you can," Holly answered, but it took a moment to get her bearings. "I should have thought of that, Dixie. You can call her anytime you like."

"Tonight?" Dixie finally looked at her. "Could I call and tell her about the horses and about Cooter?"

As if on cue, the dog bounded to Dixie's side and sat next to her, wagging his tail happily.

"Yes, definitely." Holly looked from Dixie to Colt, wanting him to say something. Daisy was his sister, after all.

He gave a quick nod. "I think that should be fine. I'm sure she'd like to talk to you."

Dixie didn't seem to notice the tension. She hugged Colt and hurried off to Isaac's side.

"She needs that connection. With Daisy, I mean," Holly spoke quietly, trying to keep the conversation between them.

"I know she does. I just..." He met her eyes. "I don't want to lose her."

"Me either, but we'll definitely lose her if we don't allow her to talk to your sister. She needs Daisy in her life."

"I know." He turned his attention back to the trailer and Isaac. "I've always loved the memory of that baby girl, with her cry that sounded like a kitten and those big dark eyes. But it was a lifetime ago. It's almost like it belonged to another person. This girl, she's more than a memory, and I didn't know I could love her as much as I do. She's part of us, Holly. She's all good, like you, and a little ornery like me. I don't want to let her go."

Holly leaned into him, just enough to share the moment because he'd put into words what she'd been feeling. What she couldn't tell him was that she feared losing them both. The only thing truly tying them together was Dixie—and the possibility of her staying in Hope. With them.

Colt stood there, thinking he'd forgotten something. He glanced at his watch, then jumped. "Our dinner! I'm going to take the stuff off the grill and wrap it in foil. Be right back."

"Why don't you let me do that? I can't help Isaac but I can take care of dinner." Holly started to head in that direction.

"You're sure?"

She nodded and hightailed it to the house like her feet were on fire.

"Are you going to help?" Isaac yelled at him from across the yard. Colt saw Dixie standing on the side of the trailer petting the golden nose that protruded from the window.

A car pulled down the drive. Jack's car. Obviously coming to get his fair share of hugs for the gift he'd given.

"It's Grandpa Jack!" Dixie hopped off the side of the trailer and ran over to wait for Jack to pull up.

Colt joined Isaac, who had stepped into the trailer and was backing the first horse out, a big bay with a deep red color and black socks, his black tail flagged, hinting at Arabian blood.

He took the lead rope from Isaac. "That's a lot of horse," he told his brother.

Isaac shrugged. "He's got spirit but he's gentle. Holly can handle him."

"I'm trusting you on that," Colt warned. "I'll put him in a stall until Holly gets back." "

"Does that barn have a stall that isn't falling apart?" Isaac asked as he walked back into the trailer.

"It's sound," Colt assured him. "I checked it out, cleaned a couple of stalls and swept out the tack room. Sure, it could use some repairs, but it won't fall in."

He led the horse into the first stall and opened the door of the next stall for Isaac as he led the light gold palomino into the barn. The horse snorted and stomped as he sniffed his new domain.

Colt looked the animal over. "Is that a kid's horse? He seems pretty flighty."

Jack, Dixie and Maria joined them in the barn, and Dixie hurried over to the palomino.

"He's a kid's horse," Jack answered. "I rode him myself."

Colt's eyes widened at that. "*You* rode him?"

"He did," Isaac said. "I found out after the fact."

"I'm old but I can still outride both of you." Jack turned his attention to Colt. "I hand-picked that gelding for my granddaughter. I rode him, and Isaac rode him when I got him back to the ranch. He's seven years old, been used for pole bending and barrels, as well as Western pleasure in local showdeos."

Colt nodded. "I believe you. He just seemed a little fiery."

"He's in new surroundings," Jack shot back. "How do you like him, Dixie Bell?"

All smiles, Dixie ran to hug her grandfather, almost knocking him off his feet. Quickly she steadied him.

"I think he's the most beautiful horse ever. Thank you, Granddad."

Granddad? Colt never thought hearing his dad called "granddad" would do something funny to his own heart.

Jack dropped a kiss on the top of her head. "Have your uncle Isaac take him out to that overgrown corral and lunge him a bit. There should be a long rope in the tack section of that trailer that is used for lunging. Isaac can show you how that works and then you can see how he rides."

"I can ride him? Really?" Dixie looked from Jack to Colt.

"He's yours, so I guess you can." Colt limped to the trailer and brought out a lunge line. He tossed it to Isaac. "Do the honors."

"Will do, gimpy." Isaac laughed as he sidestepped Colt.

Holly joined them a few minutes later. She

hugged Jack and then Maria before joining Colt as they walked out to the arena.

"Do you want to try your horse?" Colt asked as they stood together at the wood fence of the corral.

"Maybe later, after dinner." She watched as Isaac helped Dixie saddle her horse.

Jack watched, too, but then he ambled over to Holly's side. "I have a proposition for you, Holly."

"Jack, you've done more than enough. The horses are beautiful. I can't begin to thank you enough for them."

He waved off the thank-you. "I have men who need to keep busy. I'd like to send them over here to clean up your fence lines, shore up that barn and paint your house."

Tears filled her eyes. Colt wanted to thank his dad for the offer, and also warn him to tread lightly. He didn't get the chance.

"I can't let you do that, Jack." She kissed him on the cheek. "But thank you for the offer."

Jack gave her a stern look. "Holly Carter, your stubbornness doesn't make it easy to help you. I'd really like to be a good neighbor and a good friend, and I'd really like to do this for you."

"Let him, Holly," Colt told her.

"And Colt is going to be in charge of making sure it all gets done." Jack grinned as he reached for the fence to steady himself.

"I have a café to run," Colt informed his dad.

"I thought you were the silent partner," Jack shot back.

"Yeah, that's me. The loudest silent partner ever," Colt cracked.

Jack's expression turned to amusement. "That's pretty sneaky of you both." He looked at Holly. "I'll send my construction foreman over at the beginning of the week so he can look around, get an idea of what needs to be done."

"Look!" Dixie called from the arena. She had her horse saddled. Jack's offer and Holly's refusal were forgotten.

Colt had no intention of missing this. He opened a nearby gate and entered the arena to join his daughter and Isaac.

Isaac smiled. "I didn't think you'd stand idly by and let me be the one to teach her to ride."

"She already knows how to ride," Colt informed his know-it-all half brother. "Daisy has horses."

"Gotcha." Isaac stepped back and waved him on. "Go ahead."

"Check the girth strap," Colt told his daughter. "Make sure it's still tight."

She flipped the stirrup over the seat of the saddle and gave the strap a good pull. He let her try and then he gave the strap another good pull. Just in case. They secured the strap and he released the stirrup for her.

"Need help?" he asked.

The horse stood as still as a statue, true to Jack's opinion of him. The gelding definitely knew he belonged to a child.

"I got this," she informed him. And she did. She got her foot in the stirrup, grabbed the saddle horn and the reins, and swung her right leg over the horse's back as she pulled herself up.

"You know how to rein him, right?" Colt asked.

She placed the reins on the horse's neck, to the left side moving him right and to the right side moving him left.

"Take him around the arena. Get used to each other and don't do anything I wouldn't do," Colt told his daughter as he gave the horse a gentle pat on the rump. The gelding didn't flinch but instead waited for his rider to give the cue.

Isaac patted Colt on the back but didn't say anything. Who knew Isaac would grow up to be the softhearted one? Colt shook his head, dumbfounded by the realization.

The two of them moved to the side of the corral and watched as Dixie rode her horse, a big grin on her face. Colt guessed he probably wore a matching grin. This was something a man could get used to. Family surrounding him, taking up space in what he was coming to realize had been a pretty lonely existence.

And Holly. She stood on the outside of the wood-fenced corral, sharing a story with his dad. She laughed, and the sound meant so much because she seemed to laugh so seldom. He made a note to himself to make her laugh more often, to make her cry less.

He knew now, she was the prize he'd always been chasing after. All these years, he'd thought the money, the glory of his job, the traveling, would erase her from his memory.

He was wrong.

Chapter Eleven

Colt glanced at the calendar that hung on the office wall at the café. It was Thursday and they were closing in on the end of April. One week left of what had been a pretty crazy month. Maybe the best month of his life. Possibly the most difficult. Running the café had definitely been a learning experience. What he'd learned was that it was a lot of hard work.

The afternoon lull had hit and he walked out the office door and saw his brother Carson sitting at a corner table looking over some papers. Must be the afternoon lull at the West Medical Practice, too. Colt sat down across from him and picked up the glass of water he'd carried over.

Carson looked over the top of his black-framed glasses.

"Need something?" Carson asked.

"I was going to ask you the same. You're on my turf. Temporary turf, but still mine."

Carson closed the notebook he'd been looking over and sat back, reaching for the sugar. He poured a steady stream in his coffee mug and stirred.

"Ain't you man enough to drink your coffee black?" Colt teased.

"Is black coffee a prerequisite for being a real man?" Carson asked.

"You know I don't know big words like that." Colt passed his brother the creamer. "Here, you might need this."

"Let's not play the 'Colt is stupid' game. We know you have degree in marketing. I think you even went back to school for something else business related?"

"That's me, the overachiever." Colt said. "Comes from having a stepfather who claimed I wouldn't amount to anything. I might not've, but that was enough to put a burr under my saddle."

"Speaking of saddles, how's Dixie doing with Flash?"

Colt felt a whole lot of pride bubble up.

"I'm heading home now to help her practice for the shindig next weekend."

"What's she entering?"

"Pole bending and Western pleasure. And possibly the egg relay."

Carson smiled. "I'm glad she's adjusting. And still seeing Kylie. How about you? Are you adjusting to family life?"

"I don't need a therapist, if that's what you're asking."

Carson's face went serious. "So big strong cowboys can't get help if they need it?"

"Not saying that, I'm just saying I'm good. I've got this handled." Unless Dixie chose Daisy. The thought of her leaving them brought an instant pain to his heart.

And then he thought about his job and leaving her and Holly… That left him even more unsettled.

"What's that look for?" Carson asked.

"Dixie has been talking to Daisy. They're close and Dixie misses her. Every time the phone rings and it's Daisy, I can see the look on Holly's face. She's worried that our daughter will choose her aunt over us. We've both talked and we get it. She's known Daisy her whole life. She associates Daisy with Becky."

"That makes sense."

"I know it makes sense but it doesn't make it any easier. On me or Holly."

Carson studied him for a moment, the pragmatic brother, always thinking things through. "I don't want to sound clichéd but you know this is going to work out, right? I know you all will do the right thing for her. Between you and me, I kinda worry about Daisy. She's a loose cannon."

"I know she is."

"Do you know anything about twins?" Carson asked.

"Not a thing. We talk, she sticks to easy topics, and Dixie."

"Maybe we should go visit when things settle down," Carson suggested. "She usually puts me off if I suggest stopping by or her coming here. We might have to make it a surprise visit."

"You know there are two things our little sister isn't fond of. One is surprises. The other is…us."

"Yeah, I'm well aware of that," Carson answered.

"And don't worry, I was listening to your advice. I know this will work out. I just hope it doesn't hurt too much in the process of working out."

"Just know that you have family and we're here for you all. We're also counting on you participating on the ranch team next week."

"Is that a fact?"

"It is." Carson grinned, then he shuffled all his paperwork together. "I just came in to have a cup of coffee with you, so I guess I'll go now."

All righty then. Colt pushed to his feet, grimacing as the muscles in his back tightened. Carson gave him that doctor look.

"You okay?"

"It depends on what you mean by okay. I'm healing up from a head-on accident with a one-ton bull. If that wasn't bad enough, now I'm working as a waiter and dishwasher. I'd rather go out and load about a thousand square bales of hay. I think it would be easier."

"If you need anything, let me know. And practice your branding skills."

"Branding?"

Carson walked away, grinning.

"I'm not branding!" Colt called to his brother's back. The only response was a wave and a deep chuckle.

Stacy appeared from the kitchen, drying her hands on a towel. "When is that new dishwasher showing up? I fought against it but now I'm looking forward to it."

"I got an email that it should be delivered next week." He glanced at his watch. "I'm going to hit the road, if you've got things handled for the dinner shift."

"We've got this. Jess is coming in to wait tables. We have plenty of help."

"Thanks, Stacy. I mean it. I don't know what we would have done without you."

"Holly needed some time off." Stacy shrugged. "I get it. She didn't say a word when I took off for an appendectomy. She pulled the sled pretty much on her own."

And he hadn't known. Guilt felt like a lead weight in the pit of his stomach. "That won't happen again. Even after I leave, I'll make sure I keep in contact and when she needs help or time off, I'll be here."

Stacy gave him an approving smile. "I think that's good. I'm glad she's letting you help out. But I didn't know you planned on leaving."

"I guess none of us really know what's going to happen in the next few weeks," he answered. "I have events on the calendar that I've committed to."

"I see." But the look on her face said she didn't. "None of my business."

"I'm going to head home now." No, he corrected himself, not home. He was heading to Holly's. Home for him was a brick house a mile down the road from Holly's. His home had been furnished, decorated and left empty. He slept there. He had his horse there. It definitely didn't feel like home.

Pulling up to Holly's house a few minutes later felt like coming home. When he saw his daughter and Holly working with their horses, his heart skipped a beat. Most men searched for fame, for fortune, for success, but this, this was living. Stepping out of his truck, he heard his daughter call out a greeting and watched a smile shift the smooth planes of Holly's face.

He headed their way, walking easier now than he had in a long time, even after the long shift at the café. He knew he smelled like fried food but he didn't really care. He wanted to be near them.

"What are you two up to?" he asked, reaching to pet Cooter, who moved from where he'd been sprawled in the grass and came to sit at Colt's side.

"Working. I'm doing a lot better at barrels."

She turned her horse in the direction of the starting point. "Watch."

"I will. Let me get my timer ready." He leaned against the top of the fence and Holly led her horse out to stand next to him.

"Ready." He looked up at her and she smiled big. "Set." The horse started to prance and his rider looked about to go off. "Go."

Horse and rider flew around the first barrel, on to the second, touching but not knocking it down. They skidded around the third barrel and headed home with Dixie leaning over her horse's neck.

"That was awesome," he shouted. "This is a smaller corral and the barrels are closer together but that came in at twenty-five seconds."

"Is that good?"

Colt laughed at her enthusiasm. "Yes, it's very good. Now it's Holly's turn."

"I can't barrel race," she argued.

"Why not?"

"I'm too old for this. I've never done it before."

"Oh come on, Mom." Dixie looked from Colt to Holly, then smiled shyly. "That wasn't so bad, was it? I mean, you *are* my mom."

Holly drew in a breath and gave her a shaky

nod. "I am, but I don't want you to do something you're not comfortable with."

She wanted to be the mom. That's what Colt knew. Just as he wanted to be the dad. It felt like a crazy, jumbled-up mess with the three of them trying to figure out who they were to one another. But never quite getting there.

"Will you try it?" Dixie continued, as if she needed to fill the silence. "I've never done it before, either. We could both enter. Like a…" She bit down on her bottom lip. "Like a mother-daughter thing."

"Okay, I'll give it a try," Holly agreed.

Colt touched her back and she smiled over her shoulder at him as she led her horse into the arena. She was fine, the look said. Nothing to worry about. Nothing to cry over. He knew her so well, that was what she would be telling herself at that moment.

As she prepared to ride, a truck came up the drive. His troublesome brother, Isaac.

"Whenever you're ready," Colt called out to Holly. "Remember to use your knees and lean in, don't fight your horse."

"Don't fight your horse," she repeated. "That helps a lot."

"Trot the first time," Isaac offered.

"Trot." She clucked and let the horse take off, guiding him from barrel to barrel.

"Isn't it fun?" Dixie called out.

"If you like bouncing your teeth out of your head," Holly answered.

"Let him canter, it's an easier gait." Colt stepped through the gate. "Well, little brother, what brings you by?"

"I thought I'd see if Dixie wanted to come over and hang out with Allie for a bit. We're making ice cream and it's almost done."

"And you're not inviting us?" Colt looked back at his brother.

"Nope, I'm not. I thought maybe the two of you…"

Could use some time alone. Just the two of them. Colt silently thanked his brother for being thoughtful. He would have voiced his thanks but he guessed Rebecca was the thoughtful one.

Not that it mattered whose idea it was. The end result was the same, unless Holly objected: the two of them would have a little time alone.

"Go!" Dixie called out.

Holly's horse shot forward, seeming to know what he was doing and thinking Holly was along for the ride. Which she guessed might be the truth. But she wanted to hang on for the ride and not land on the ground. She didn't have time to remind herself to lean or to use her knees. Her horse was named Blue, as in Blue Streak, though he was red. That was her last thought as she tumbled from the saddle, hit the barrel and landed on the ground.

Cooter barked and Dixie screamed the word *Momma*. Momma was a good name. Stretched out on her back, she looked up at the late-afternoon sky, which was blue. Robin's-egg blue.

She heard boots on the ground come closer. Colt said her name. She smiled up at him. "I'm fine."

"Are you? Because you're lying on the ground and you haven't moved." He sounded concerned.

Should he be? She didn't know. "I'm not moving because I'm looking at the sky. And Dixie called me Momma."

"Yes, she did. But right now, we need to make sure you're all right."

"What day is today?" Isaac asked from his position on her other side.

She laughed and found that laughing made

her ribs hurt. "I don't know what day it is, because I no longer have a job. The days all run together."

With Colt's hand on her back, she moved to a sitting position. Her head spun a little, but then it settled down. "That isn't the ride I wanted to take," she said with her forehead on her knees.

A smaller hand touched her shoulder. "Are you sure you're okay?"

The tremulous quality in that young voice shifted things. Holly raised her head and smiled at her daughter. Dixie mattered more than a bruised shoulder or an ache in her ribs.

"Of course I'm fine." Holly managed what she hoped was her best smile. "I'm good. I just need to get up off the ground and apologize to my horse for doing something I have no business doing."

Dixie gave her a lopsided grin. "You were doing pretty good."

"Was I?"

Dixie nodded, looking younger than her years, more vulnerable. More in need of Holly. Colt stood next to her now, offering to help her up. She took it, standing with care. He gave her a discerning look.

"Everything feel okay?" he asked.

"Sore but nothing broken." She wrapped an arm around Dixie and pulled her close, dropping a kiss on the top of her head. "I love you."

"I love you, too." Thin but strong arms wrapped around Holly's waist. And around her heart.

Isaac cleared his throat. "Now that Holly's trick riding clinic is over, I'm going back to my house. And leave the three of you to your dinner."

"Ice cream?" Colt interjected.

Dixie looked from Colt to Isaac.

"She can still join us, if she wants to." Isaac looked to Dixie. "If she wants. I know Allie would love it if she'd come over and hang out for a bit."

"Are you sure you're okay?" Dixie asked Holly. "Because if you are, I'm going to go hang out with Allie and have ice cream."

"I'm positive I'm okay," Holly told her with a quick hug. "Go and have fun. What about your horse?"

"Already fed and in the field."

"One of us will bring her back later," Isaac told them in parting.

Then they were gone and Holly was left standing in the arena with Colt. He'd retrieved her horse's reins, the animal having stopped a few feet away to graze.

"Now what?" Holly asked as she watched Isaac's truck pull away.

"Let's take care of your horse first, then we'll have dinner." He walked next to her, leading the horse. "Just the two of us."

"Did you arrange all this?"

"Me? Arrange for Isaac to take our daughter for the evening? Why would you ever think I'd do something like that?"

She didn't know if she should be aggravated or honored.

"I don't know, but it does seem convenient that you made an amazing meal, and then Isaac suddenly shows up."

"As much as I'd like to claim responsibility, it was all Isaac and Rebecca," he admitted.

They left the corral and walked through the wide double doors of the barn. Colt tied her horse to a ring on the wall and took care of the animal while she sat on a nearby stool. As he brushed the horse out, he gave her a careful look.

"You're sure?" he began.

"I'm sure. I'm sore and bruised but I'm not broken."

"It scared me," he said as he put the brush in a nearby bucket.

She stood as he led the horse out of the barn.

"Why would you be scared?" she asked as he turned the horse into the field. The gelding trotted across the green grass, his black tail held high. His gait was showy as he pranced, raising his front legs high.

"Why my dad ever got you an Arab, I will never know," he said, shaking his head.

"I know, you're a quarter horse man. Personally, I like my guy. He's sweet and he has class. But he's not a barrel horse."

"No, he is definitely *not* a barrel horse."

She reached for his hand and they walked across the lawn toward the house hand in hand. "You've seen plenty of people getting thrown from horses and you've been thrown plenty. Don't blame the horse—it happens."

They were standing near an old oak tree, gnarled with time, damaged by the Oklahoma winds. He pulled her close, taking her by surprise. And his shudder as he released a breath nearly undid her emotions that she held so carefully in check, protecting them from this man who could devastate her so easily.

It had taken a long time for her to get to a

place where she felt strong, where she didn't miss him, where she didn't hurt because he'd so easily left her for someone else.

As his hands sifted through her hair, making her feel as if there could never be anyone else, she tried to remind herself of the past. Standing there with him, a gentle breeze swirling around them, rustling the new leaves in the ancient oak, she couldn't think about the past. Not today. Today wasn't a day for the past. It was all about the present.

With an impatient motion he jerked off his hat and lowered his mouth to touch hers, brushing ever so gently before claiming her in a heartrending kiss. She brushed her hand across his cheek and trailed her fingers through the dark strands of hair at the back of his neck.

After a minute she regained her senses and backed out of his embrace. Out of his arms was a lonely place to be. He scrubbed a hand across his stubbly cheek and bent to retrieve the hat he'd dropped.

"You make me forget myself," he told her. "It's always been that way."

"Except when it was someone else," she muttered, feeling the heat climb into her cheeks. "I'm sorry, that isn't what this moment calls for. Because really, as far as kisses go, that one was spectacular."

"Should I say thank you or apologize?" He pushed his hat down on his head and Holly gave him a quick look, this cowboy of hers with his faded jeans and scuffed up boots.

He wasn't truly hers, was he?

"It's time we talk about it, Holly." He took her by the hand and led her up the steps to the back door.

"I don't know." Walking through the door he opened for her, she looked around the familiar kitchen of the home she'd grown up in. A kitchen that his presence filled. He'd cooked a fantastic dinner. He moved about the room as if he'd always been here, in her home, in her life.

His expression darkened as he went to pull a knife out and began to cut the meat, moving it to a platter once it was done.

She then noticed that there were candles on the dining room table. "No, let's not talk about it. Not tonight."

"We have to or it will always be between us. That day when you were so hurt and you had so much to say, and I laughed at you and told you that life was never fair...that was not a man I was proud of."

"I didn't particularly care for him, either. And I promised myself that day that I wouldn't fall in love again. I wouldn't let you or anyone else ever hurt me that way."

"Smart move. I know I'm not the most upstanding guy but I'm sorry for that day. I'm sorry I hurt you. I hope you'll forgive me for the man I was and give the man I am now a chance to prove his worth."

She looked at the table, with the single rose in a vase and the candles that hadn't been lit yet. She felt his hand touch her shoulder. The room turned orange and pink as the sun began to sink on the western horizon.

"I want to trust you," she whispered, his nearness unsettling.

"I know and I don't expect it to be easy."

"The problem with trust is that there's more to our story now. We have a daughter. You have a career that'll take you on the road. It's all of these shifting, changing pieces and none of them seem to fit together."

"It does seem that way," he told her. He kissed her hair, and the gesture was warm and somehow comforting.

"So what do we do?"

"I don't know," he answered with painful honesty.

"Me either." She turned, wrapping her arms around him and resting her head on his shoulder. "But I'm not going to let it ruin our dinner. I want to move forward. I want to have a friendship with you because our daughter deserves that."

"Just friendship?" he asked.

She knew what he meant. When he kissed her, it felt beyond friendship. It felt as if their mutual past disappeared and they were discovering each other as two adults.

And spectacular kisses. She couldn't forget those kisses.

But a kiss didn't make forever. A kiss didn't mean they could be more than friends. A kiss simply made it all more complicated.

But for now, at least they were heading in the right direction.

Chapter Twelve

Holly left the women's fellowship lunch on Friday, walking outside the church building to a sunny day that signaled the first week of May had arrived with warm weather and blue skies. Perfect weather for the showdeo that was coming up tomorrow. Hopefully the good weather held.

She hadn't been to Bible study in years, and it had been nice to sit with the other women, talk about the book of Ephesians, share prayer requests and discuss upcoming events at church.

Isaac's wife Rebecca had asked if they could pray about the situation with Dixie, and it had been overwhelming to have those women join hands with her and pray for God's wisdom and His plan for her daughter. The coming weeks would be difficult as the time grew near when they had to make a more permanent decision about Dixie's guardianship.

Even when Dixie called her Mom, Holly knew that Daisy was out there somewhere, tugging on her child's heart without even trying. The longer Dixie stayed, though, the more she adjusted to a life in Hope with Holly.

And Colt.

As she walked to the café, Rebecca caught up with her.

"Hey, I'll walk with you." Rebecca smoothed a hand over her belly. "Any day now."

Holly felt a twinge of envy but quickly pushed it aside. Rebecca had seen her own share of troubles, having her daughter Allie when she was barely out of high school. Her move to Hope had brought her more than hope, it had brought Isaac West into their lives. And now they were expanding their family.

"How are you feeling?" Holly asked as she slowed her steps for the other woman.

"Huge," Rebecca laughed. "And ready to have this baby out of me. How are things going with Dixie?"

She shrugged. "Good, I think. Sometimes

calls us Mom and Dad, sometimes just Holly and Colt. But I know she still misses Broken Arrow. She misses her school and her friends, and most of all, Daisy. They talk on the phone, but that isn't the same."

"Daisy won't visit?" Rebecca asked as she headed for a bench in the park. "Sorry, I need a break to catch my breath."

Holly sat next to her. "Daisy doesn't want to visit Hope, but she said she's going to think about it. She has a lot going on with her businesses and in her personal life."

"Are you afraid Dixie will choose Daisy instead of you?" Rebecca asked. Then her expression softened. "I'm sorry, I don't mean to pry, I just know how I would feel."

"I don't think Dixie knows what she wants, not really. And even if she stays with us, Colt and I will have to come up with some shared custody agreement that we can take before a judge to convince them we're suitable parents. What we're doing seems to work right now and maybe it would work for the future. With Colt just a mile away, we're able to share meals, spend Sundays together and hang out. But then when he goes back to work, that'll be a whole new problem. He will be on the road a lot, and only come home when he gets a chance."

Rebecca moved the hand from her belly and reached for Holly's hand. "I'm so sorry. If you need anything—a friend, a cup of coffee, someone to talk to—I'm here."

"Thank you, Rebecca." Holly gave her hand a squeeze. "That means a lot."

The two of them continued their slow walk to Lakeside Drive where shops lined the streets, and on this Friday in May, cars filled all the parking spaces. They were almost to the café when a red convertible turned a corner and zoomed into an empty parking spot that had just been vacated.

The woman, dark hair held at bay by a colorful scarf, hopped out of the car. She pulled off her dark sunglasses and looked around, at once confident and nervous. She bit down on her bottom lip, the bright red of her lipstick a contrast to her dark hair.

Holly stopped, suddenly all too aware of who had just driven into town. She put a hand on Rebecca's arm, needing an anchor.

"What's wrong?" Fairly new to the family, Rebecca probably hadn't experienced this particular Oklahoma storm.

"Daisy." She tilted her head in the direction of the woman and her red car.

"Oh, my. That's a surprise."

Holly summoned her courage, telling herself this didn't have to be bad news for any of them. She continued up the sidewalk, pasting a bright smile on her face. A long time ago, she and Daisy had been friends. Daisy was younger by a couple of years, but they'd played together as children.

"I'll go with you," Rebecca insisted, remaining at her side.

"You don't have to. I know you need to get back to the salon."

"I'm going with you." Rebecca was petite and quiet, but loyal. Holly had always liked her but now she realized that Rebecca was a true friend, not just someone who came to the café or someone she bumped into at church.

Daisy noticed them. She hitched her handbag over her shoulder and waited for them to approach. Even standing there on a sidewalk in Hope, Daisy was poised. She appeared confident, as if she knew how to bend the world to her bidding. But Holly wasn't convinced. No one could be that confident.

"Holly," Daisy greeted as they approached.

"And Rebecca. You're looking beautiful these days."

Rebecca hugged Daisy as if the two were old friends. "It is so good to see you. I can't believe you're in Hope."

"I know, I'm just as surprised." Daisy did a sidestep as a group of men walked by. One of them stopped, whistled and backed up.

"Daisy Duke, is that you?" David Brant didn't have a shy bone in his body. "I haven't seen you in twenty years, but I'd recognize you anywhere."

She slid the sunglasses to the top of her head and gave him a sideways look. "David?"

"The one and only." He grinned, all cute and cowboy with too much confidence.

"Fortunate for the rest of us. The world couldn't handle two of you."

"Have you forgotten, I have a twin?"

"Jonathan. How could I forget that your mother named you after Bible characters? You're like a living Old Testament story come to life."

"That's us. How long are you in town?"

"Not long," she answered, her attention shifting back to Holly. "Nice seeing you."

He was charming but he could also take a hint. "See you around?"

She smiled but didn't answer.

"Dixie is in school right now," Holly told her.

"I thought she might be," Daisy said. "It's Friday."

"Yes," Holly responded. She stood there unsure of what to do or say next.

"Why don't we go in for a cup of coffee?" Rebecca took control, turning them toward the front of the café. "If I stand here much longer, Baby West is going to be born on this sidewalk."

Daisy thawed at the mention of the baby. "How much longer?"

"Days. Weeks. Who knows really when he'll decide to make his entrance?" Rebecca pushed the front door open, sighing as they entered the air-conditioned café. "Much better."

"Except for the audience." Daisy glanced around, uneasy. "Maybe this wasn't such a great idea."

"We can use the back dining room. It's empty," Holly told her.

"That would be perfect. I'd rather not be on display."

"You're home for the first time in years."

Rebecca patted her arm in a motherly way. "People are going to stare."

"They just want to see the scar."

"Nonsense," Rebecca told her. "What scar?"

Daisy laughed, although it wasn't with amusement. "Keep telling yourself that. Or maybe I should say, keep telling *me* that."

Holly closed the doors that separated the back room from the front of the café. Daisy had moved to a table at the back of the room, as if she couldn't get far enough from the main dining area and the curiosity of the diners on the other side of the door.

Rebecca headed for the kitchen. "I'll get us coffee. And pie. I definitely need pie."

"Thank you," Holly said as the other woman disappeared through the door to the kitchen. She was now alone with Daisy, and everything seemed slow motion.

Daisy had taken a seat at the table and had rearranged the condiments, not looking up to face Holly. "Surprise!"

"A phone call would have been nice."

"We're not enemies, you know," Daisy murmured.

Daisy had a good point. They weren't enemies. They were two people who loved the same child. She pulled out a chair and sat next to Daisy.

"You're right," Holly answered. "We're not enemies. It's just…this is so much harder than anything I've ever had to do before. I gave her up once. I don't want to do it again."

"I know."

"But you love her, too?" Holly cleared her throat. Thinking of Dixie torn between the two of them was making her break, for Dixie and for herself. And for Daisy. It would hurt them all. "And she loves all of us. So how do we do this without hurting her? Because no matter who she chooses, I want her to feel safe in the choice, knowing we all support her and love her."

"Is that even possible? For it to not hurt." Daisy asked, smiling at Rebecca, who had reappeared with a tray laden with pie and coffee.

"Look at me being a waitress," Rebecca joked, placing the tray on the table.

Daisy smiled, seeming more at ease as she looked at her sister-in-law. "Thank you, for the pie—and for being so good for my brother."

"It's actually my pleasure." Rebecca smiled

at Daisy. "I wish we could spend more time together."

"Hmm," Daisy replied. "I'm afraid that isn't possible."

"The two of you need to talk." Rebecca didn't take a seat. Instead she took a piece of pie already in a plastic container. "Colt is finishing up an order and he'll join you. He asked me to pass the message along to you."

"Great." Daisy shuddered. "Just what we need, the big bad brother."

"He isn't," Holly began, but saying more would be too much.

"Isn't he?" Daisy said a quick goodbye to Rebecca, then picked up a fork and speared up a bite of chocolate chess pie. "I hardly think you should be the one to defend him. He did wrong by you."

"You're right. He did." The answer came from across the room. Colt took off his apron and joined them at the table. "But he's trying to do better."

"Hi, brother." Daisy gave him a cheeky grin. "Good to see you."

His expression gentled. "I'm glad to see you."

"Family reunions are so sweet," she said. "As long as this is the only family I have to see. Except for Carson's children. I adore Maggie and Adam. And obviously Dixie."

"And Jack?" Colt asked.

"No, I don't think so." She tapped her bright red fingernails on the table. "Don't push, Colt."

Colt shrugged. "Wouldn't dream of it."

"I'm here to spend the weekend with you all. I want to see Dixie. If that's okay. I miss her."

"She misses you, too," Holly offered, because it was true.

"It's hard," Daisy said, digging the fork into her pie but not taking a bite. She stared at the chocolate confection and sighed. "I don't like chocolate."

"That's not so hard," Colt said. "Just give it to me."

She slid it across the table. "That isn't what I meant and you know it."

"I know." Colt took a bite and dug in for another, as if he wasn't bothered by the situation. Holly kicked his foot.

"Ouch! What was that for?"

"Stop eating pie." Holly reached for the plate but he was too fast and took the last bite.

"I'm not sure what Becky was thinking," Colt said. "I know she thought she was giving us a chance to get to know our daughter. But I can't help think she could have done things differently, in a way that wouldn't have put this kind of pressure on Dixie."

"Maybe we should decide for her?" Daisy suggested.

"Would you decide for her or yourself?" Colt asked.

"Unfair," his sister shot back. "I love her but I wouldn't make a decision that hurt her."

"Any decision we make is going to hurt her," Holly countered.

"True," Colt and Daisy said simultaneously.

"What do we do?" Daisy asked, adjusting the bright red scarf at her throat.

Holly considered the question, knowing that there wouldn't be easy answers. "Kylie," she said. "What if Kylie helps Dixie find the best solution, and then helps us all figure out a way to do this so that Dixie has some stability and continuity in her life? None of us want to see her forced to make decisions that will hurt. But if we can find a compromise that makes Dixie feel safe?"

Daisy toyed with her cup of coffee. "Spoken like a true mother."

"I gave birth to her, Daisy. I'm only now learning how to be her mother."

"You've always been her mother. From the very beginning, making decisions that were tough but in her best interest." Daisy reached for her hand. "I know this is hard, but I want us to work together. Becky meant well but she put us all in a difficult situation."

"She did," Colt said. "But if we can work together…"

"We can," Daisy assured him.

Holly felt her heart ease. "Why don't we pick Dixie up from school together, the three of us."

Daisy nodded. "I'd like that."

Holly managed a smile but inside she felt as if her life hung by a thread. She had gotten so used to Dixie in her home and in her life. She'd gotten used to their visits to see Opal, to cooking meals together, watching movies on weekends. She'd gotten used to Colt in her life again, making her feel as if she had someone on her side, someone to lean on.

She couldn't think about what would happen in the next few weeks, when Dixie made a decision about where she wanted to live, and when Colt returned to the career he loved.

It was just too painful to contemplate.

Colt didn't know what he'd expected when the three of them pulled up to the middle school to pick up Dixie. He guessed he'd expected jubilation from his daughter. After all, she'd been begging Daisy to come see them. He hadn't expected tears as Dixie fell sobbing into Daisy's arms.

From the look on Daisy's face as she held their daughter, she hadn't expected it, either. She looked uncomfortable with the emotions, completely taken by surprise.

"We should go," Holly stated, taking control, herding them all toward his truck and off the main sidewalk where other children were passing by, staring.

Dixie managed to pull herself together, but she didn't let go of Daisy. Over and over again she told his sister she'd missed her. She wanted to see Pumpkin, Daisy's dog. She wanted to know if Daisy had her books. The dog was at a kennel for the weekend. The books were in Daisy's car, back at Holly's. Except Daisy referred to Holly as Dixie's mom. Another surprise.

"You're going to stay and go to the showdeo? I'm going to be in it." Dixie held on to Daisy's hand, letting go only to climb in the back seat of his truck.

"I'll stay but I don't think I can go to the

showdeo." Daisy looked to Colt for help. He got it. She didn't want to see Jack.

She needed to see their father. But it wasn't his place to tell her what to do. He'd been through that and knew that life got a little easier after confronting the past. His little sister would have to figure that out on her own.

At least Daisy had seen Jack when he was in the hospital a couple of years ago. Maybe she considered that enough.

A few minutes later he parked under the shade of an oak tree at Holly's. Dixie dragged Daisy out of the car and over to the barn, telling her she just had to meet Cooter and Flash. She had to see the new kittens, too. Daisy went along with Dixie, allowing herself to be led to the barn. Cooter joined them, sniffing at their hands and barking when Dixie tossed a stick for him to fetch.

Holly took Colt's hand and stopped him when he meant to follow them. "Let them go," she said.

"But what if Daisy tries to convince her to go?"

Her hand tightened on his. "She won't. And if she does, what can we really do about it?"

"Get a lawyer and fight her," he said, not truly meaning it. "Years ago I let you down. If not for me, we might have been a family. You might have had her with you all these years. I don't want you to lose her again."

"I'm not going to lose her again. No matter what she decides, I know I'll always be in her life, a part of her world."

He pulled her close. He had never felt as whole as he did now, with her at his side. "I know you're right but man, I don't want to let her go."

"We aren't. We're letting her find her own way. And Kylie can continue to help, too." She led him to an old glider swing on the front porch and they sat together. "I'm trying very hard to find peace."

"I'm trying very hard to fix things for you," he laughed. "In case you haven't noticed, I'm not very good at letting go."

"I know, I'm the same way. We both like to control our situations. But true faith requires us to trust God's plan."

"I want you to trust me," Colt told her as they sat together, the warm afternoon sun beating down on them. In the distance cattle mooed and a car honked. Other than that it was a quiet spot where they could see the green of the country for miles without much more than a barn in the distance.

"Trust you?"

He chuckled a little. "Not that I'm taking away from the Good Lord. I know He has this all under control. I mean on a personal level, trust me."

"I'm working on that," she told him as she watched their daughter. "Don't take it personally, it's just... I've been on my own for a very long time. I've learned to trust God, but to only rely on myself. It isn't easy for me, broadening the circle of trust."

"I know. Especially when I abused your trust in the worst way. I just want you to see that I'm not the man I was."

"I know."

He watched as Dixie led Daisy through the field. Even from a distance he could hear bits and pieces of her excited chatter. He smiled, because how could he not?

"She's a lot like you." Holly spoke after a few minutes. "Full of life. She makes friends easily. I have to look a little deeper to see myself in her."

"Always the caretaker," Colt answered. "I don't have to look too hard to see that side of her."

"It's something I never expected." Holly watched her daughter, now on the back of her horse, bareback, as Daisy led her around the pasture. The wind whipped at the horse's mane, and Dixie leaned down to hug the animal's neck.

"What's that?" Colt asked.

"I always pictured her as the infant we held. Yes, I got pictures from Becky, but those pictures were of a little girl I didn't know. They were one-dimensional. Now that she's here with us, I see every side of her. She loves math but doesn't like history. She draws horses and wants to learn to knit. She laughs like you and sometimes smiles like Opal."

"She's all of us," Colt agreed. "And she's Becky, too. The side of her that is thinking through this situation and the girl who can't leave a dirty dish on the counter."

Holly laughed at that. "She didn't get that from me. Or from you."

"No, she didn't."

Dixie and Daisy made their way back to the barn and Colt got up, holding a hand out for Holly. She took it, surprising him.

Yes, they were friends. They could parent together. But this connection went beyond their friendship, beyond parenting Dixie.

He wanted more.

He wanted Holly in his life forever.

Chapter Thirteen

The Hope Saddle Club Arena was bright from stadium lights and buzzed with activity and conversations and music. The aroma of burgers being cooked on a grill wafted through the evening air, drawing hungry crowds to line up at the concession stand. It was the first Saturday in May and the opening of the show and rodeo season. There would be Western pleasure classes, saddle bronc riding, team roping, pole bending, barrel racing and a ranch event with teams from local ranches.

From where Holly'd been sitting on the bleachers, she headed to the back lot where horse trailers were parked in rows. Horses whinnied and people gathered in groups, talking and laughing. In an area roped off to keep cars from parking too close, a bandstand and dance floor had been set up.

She saw the two trailers with the Mercy Ranch brand emblazoned on the side and soon spotted Kylie and Carson with a group of residents from the ranch.

Smiling, Kylie waved her over. "Come join us and listen to the men argue about who is doing what on the ranch teams."

It had been years since Holly had been to a rodeo, and she couldn't remember if she'd ever seen a rodeo where teams from local ranches competed in events that simulated normal ranch activities.

"What are the events in the ranch rodeo portion?" Holly asked.

"I'm not completely sure, but I did hear something about milking a wild cow." Kylie grinned as she filled her in. "And I can only imagine how that will go. I think there's a team penning event, too. That won't be nearly as amusing for me."

"Should be fun," Holly answered as she scanned the crowd for her daughter.

"That was less than enthusiastic," Kylie noted. "How's it going with Daisy?"

Holly shrugged a shoulder. "It seems all right."

"But?"

"But I guess we just have to wait and see. Dixie's thrilled to have Daisy here and I can see that they are very close."

Suddenly, she spied them walking back from an open lot, Daisy leading Flash and Dixie next to her. They were laughing and talking; Daisy leaned her head down to catch something Dixie said.

Holly shrugged again. "I don't want to be envious of their relationship. They've known each other for years. I'm really just a stranger who shares Dixie's DNA."

Kylie gave her a quick hug. "You're so much more than that and you know it. In the past few weeks, the two of you have gotten to know each other. It does take time but don't discount that DNA you share."

"I know, and thank you for everything you've done for us."

"You know I'm always here." Kylie glanced around. "Oh, I need to find Rebecca. I left Maggie and Adam with her. Also, before I go, I love my brother-in-law dearly, but get back to the café soon. We miss you there."

"I'm planning on returning Monday. He hasn't said anything, but I think he's ready to rehire me."

Kylie gave her a thoughtful look. "I do think he's really enjoying himself."

"As long as he doesn't want to take over permanently." Then she admitted the truth. "The break has been good for me. I needed the time with Dixie but also time to rest."

"Being a caretaker is exhausting, Holly. I wish I'd said something or offered help sooner. We all get busy with our lives and fail to see the need around us."

"You don't have to feel guilty, Kylie. I would have asked for help if I'd needed it."

Kylie arched a brow at that. "Really?"

Holly paused for a moment. "Okay, maybe not."

"Most caretakers won't ask for help. It's up to friends and family to step in from time to time. I just want you to know that I am here and I want to do better as a friend."

"Thank you." Holly choked the words out. "Now you're making me cry."

"I didn't mean to. Please hurry back to the café. Colt is many things, but he's a lousy waitress."

Giggling as they swiped the tears from their cheeks and parted, Holly headed for the back of the arena, eager to be with Dixie.

She spotted Dixie and Daisy with a group

of other young riders. It was a scene that Holly had witnessed more than once in her life. She'd never been a part of this crowd, just a spectator. Tonight she felt like a spectator once again as she watched her daughter and Daisy chatting together with the other contestants. She took a deep breath as she approached and reminded herself that Dixie needed her here.

Just then, Colt materialized. She watched as he stepped up to check Dixie's saddle. He said something to her and they all laughed. He was her kryptonite, her weakness, this cowboy in his dark blue plaid shirt, a white cowboy hat and faded jeans. He looked rugged, handsome, confident and happy. She wanted to believe in him, to trust him, to have him in her life from now on.

The problem was, her memories were full of a man who cheated on her. Of growing up hearing lectures from her mom that men couldn't be trusted. That they couldn't be counted on to be there for a woman.

Opal's Rules of Romance. But Holly knew that there *were* good men around.

But Colt was her weakness, and giving in to him could result in a broken heart.

"Mom, there you are!" Dixie waved from

the saddle of Flash, her smile huge and contagious.

Holly smiled back as she weaved through the crowd. "Of course I'm here. Where else would I be?"

"I don't know, but I was worried because I haven't seen you. I didn't want to go on without you being here."

Holly put a hand on her daughter's arm. "I'm here. I wouldn't be anywhere else. You're going to do great," she told her daughter, giving her arm a gentle squeeze before letting go and stepping back.

"Of course I am. Flash is the best." Eleven-year-old confidence shone from her face. And joy. A lot of joy.

"Don't get too sure of yourself," Colt warned. "Confidence is good. Arrogance will trip you up. Folks who are too sure of themselves stop putting out all of the effort or they make sloppy mistakes. Also, always show good sportsmanship. Always congratulate the winner and mean it. If you're the winner, be gracious."

She saluted. "Got it."

Dixie pushed her new cowboy hat down on her head and leaned to hug her dad. The hat had been a gift from her grandpa Jack, who was seated in the stands waiting to watch her first run. She toyed with the white straw hat with the pink edging around the brim. It matched her pink plaid shirt. She'd insisted on Holly buying a matching shirt, so everyone knew they were mother and daughter.

"It's almost time for your event," Colt told her as he took off his hat and hooked it on the saddle horn. "Let's pray before you go."

Dixie nodded and Colt took her hand. He reached for Holly with his free hand. Daisy took Dixie's hand on the opposite side of the horse. They bowed their heads as Colt prayed for protection, for confidence, for humility. And for a good run. They said amen and Colt grabbed his hat and placed it back on his head.

"Go get 'em," he told her, patting her horse's neck.

Dixie turned Flash in the direction of the arena, joining the other young contestants who had moved forward to await their turn. Flash fidgeted as his young rider worked to hold him steady, patting his neck and leaning to talk to him.

"Be safe," Holly called out. Not so loud as to distract, but it made her feel better to say the words.

"It's pole bending, Holly," Colt said as he took her by the hand and led her to the side of the arena where they could watch the competition.

"I know, but still…"

He smiled down at her, flashing that charming grin of his, the one that made her knees weak. She couldn't be weak tonight. She needed the truth from him. She needed to know when he was leaving. And when he'd come back.

As they waited for Dixie to take her turn in the arena, members of the West family joined them. Carson, Kylie, their children and Isaac, as well as Daisy. They all stood together, talking about Dixie's chances of winning the competition.

"She'll be fine," Colt said, seeming as if he were reassuring himself more than anyone.

"Yes, she will." Holly agreed. Dixie would be fine. They would make sure of it. Dixie wouldn't live the life Holly had, a life without a father. A life spent caring for a mother who could never take care of herself. No matter what, Dixie's life would be different than Holly's had been.

Dixie was up next and all talking ceased as her horse shot from the gate and headed for the poles that were spaced twenty-one feet apart. Dixie and Flash raced to the end of the line of poles and started their way back, weaving between the poles, turning on the last and winding back to the far end before racing straight back to the finish.

They were all yelling and cheering her on. Colt climbed the fence and waved his hat as she crossed the finish line. When he hopped off, he grabbed Holly up, spinning her in a circle before putting her down. Taking her hand, he headed with her through the crowd to congratulate their daughter. She hadn't won, but she came in third.

She was smiling and happy with the ribbon, with her horse, with her life.

Holly wanted her to always be like this, smiling and happy. She knew there would be hard times ahead for them, but tonight showed them all that there would be good times, too.

An hour later Colt shook his head and backed away from Isaac and Carson. Joe, the foreman at Mercy Ranch, stood a few feet away. Laughing. They were all laughing, so he couldn't just blame Joe. They all thought it was pretty funny.

Joe pointed to his missing arm. "It isn't like I can hold a cup and milk a cow."

"Okay, I'll give you an out on that one. But I am the guy who recently had a broken back."

"Cracked," Carson inserted in his dry way.

"That doesn't mean it didn't hurt." Colt started to walk away but Isaac stopped him.

"Come on, brother, this is all about bonding. We're family. This is what we do."

"You want me to milk a cow that's never been milked!" Colt reached for his horse's reins. "That isn't brotherly love. That's torture."

"Chicken," Joe said quietly. "I thought you liked a challenge."

"I do like a challenge," Colt shot back. "But this isn't a challenge, it's a guaranteed trip to the hospital in the back of an ambulance."

"Trust us," Isaac said, his ever-present toothpick stuck in the corner of his mouth.

Colt laughed at those sage words. "Trust you?"

"You won't have to grab the heifer or drag her around, nothing too strenuous," Carson offered.

"Just rope her and then hop down and get a squirt of milk. One squirt, Colt. The rest of us will hold her." Isaac pulled at his hat, making sure that his good ear was toward the conversation. Colt guessed that with the noise of the crowds, he had a difficult time hearing everyone.

"Fine, if this is what I have to do to prove my brotherly loyalty, so be it."

"Said like a true West," Isaac said, grinning.

Like a West. He was a West. He'd been one from the day of his birth, screaming his way into the world. "Let's go."

Despite his arguments, Colt found himself on horseback, joining Joe in a mad attempt to rope a cow that had no intentions of being their victim. After a failed attempt, Joe managed to rope her; Colt brought her around for Carson and Isaac to help subdue her. He laughed as he watched his brothers grabbing at her. He dismounted and rushed into the fray. Carson had her by the tail, Isaac by the head. She was still moving, taking them with her.

Colt moved close to her side, grabbing at her as she twisted and turned. "It'll be easy, they said. Fun, they said. This isn't fun." But he was laughing and so were they.

He managed to get the cup under her belly

and just as she gave a little kick to escape, he squirted a stream of milk into the tin cup. Ignoring the sharp pain in his leg, he hurried to the chalk circle at the front of the arena and handed the judge the cup.

They didn't win but Colt didn't care. He'd managed to milk that cow. The bonus was that he, Joe and his brothers gave back-pounding man hugs as they walked away from the arena.

He would never admit it but Isaac had been right about the bonding thing. It felt pretty good to spend this time with his family. On his way back to the trailer, he walked his horse to let himself and the animal have a break. When he reached the truck he realized he had company.

Holly sat on the lowered tailgate of his truck. The sight of her waiting there for him took his breath away. She didn't notice him and he paused to look at her. She had her head tilted up, looking at the millions of stars that glittered in the night sky. Her hair had come loose and tendrils hung around her face. He wanted to kiss her.

He sat next to her but didn't reach for her. He wanted her to know that she controlled the narrative of their relationship. Whatever she needed from him, he wanted to be the person she could count on.

"Tonight was good," she finally said.

"It was. Dixie had a good time."

"I know." Holly held her hand out and he took it. "I think we have to talk to her. About where she wants to be. I think she needs for us to be able to hear what is going on in her heart and head without being upset, because it might not be what we want to hear."

"I agree."

"It hurts," she said, sobbing. Then she leaned into him and he wrapped an arm around her, pulling her close.

"It'll be okay," he said. "We'll figure this out."

He knew better than to make promises but he wanted to promise her everything. He wanted to tell her that Dixie would choose them. He wanted to tell her that he chose her.

For now, holding Holly in his arms was enough.

Chapter Fourteen

Holly woke up Sunday morning curled on the couch with her daughter. They'd fallen asleep watching a movie, both having been exhausted by the rodeo event. She stretched, trying to relieve the kink in her neck and undo the back spasm that had woken her, and rolled off the couch. Cooter had been sleeping on the ottoman. He gave Holly an imploring look and she nodded. The dog relocated, curling up next to Dixie, who murmured in her sleep and pulled the dog close.

For a long time Holly sat on the ottoman that Cooter had abandoned. She watched as her daughter slept, thinking of all the moments she had missed. She didn't want to miss another second of Dixie's life.

Holly quietly walked to the kitchen to start

a pot of coffee and put biscuits in the oven. She spooned apple butter into a bowl and placed it in the microwave to heat. It seemed like the perfect comfort food for a morning like this one. Coffee and biscuits smothered in warm apple butter.

She heard a car coming up the drive. It was Daisy in her red convertible.

Holly poured herself a cup of coffee and watched as Daisy headed for the back door. Colt should be joining them soon. A quick glance at the clock on the stove made her realize that Daisy had arrived early.

Holly met Daisy on the patio. "Can we sit out here?"

In answer, Daisy pulled out a chair and sat down. "Does Dixie know we're having this meeting?"

"No, I wanted us all to talk before we talk to her."

Daisy placed a hand over Holly's. "I don't want to see you hurt. I think you've been hurt enough."

"I'm okay," Holly managed. "I know we will all be okay. I just want to make sure Dixie is okay."

"I promise you, we're on the same side, Holly."

Holly buried her face in her hands, then brushed her hair back from her face. "I know."

Colt's truck pulled up.

"Do you want coffee?" Holly asked Daisy, preparing to get up. She needed to move, to do something other than sit and wait for whatever this conversation would be.

"I never drink the stuff. But thank you."

Colt joined them on the porch. "Stay put and I'll get the pot and bring it out."

"Thank you." Holly smiled up at him and he placed a hand on her shoulder.

He returned with a tray holding the thermal carafe of coffee, two mugs and spoons as well as the sugar bowl and creamer. He brought hot tea for his sister.

"You're a natural at this waitressing stuff," Daisy teased her brother. "I don't know why there have been so many complaints around town."

"Maybe because people don't like to wear their sweet tea?" Colt offered.

They shared a laugh, then the three grew serious because they all knew this wasn't about sharing work stories; this was about Dixie and her future.

"Why don't we cut to the chase?" Daisy

said. "I'd rather not sit here and pretend we're all happy with the situation Becky put us in."

"I think she had the best intentions," Holly offered. "But I don't know that this is the best thing for Dixie. She's trying to adjust and I think in time she will, but to be pulled away from everything and everyone she's known and loved and placed with strangers... I can't imagine how that feels. I had a chaotic childhood but I always had my grandmother. I had that stability."

"I don't think that Dixie lacks stability," Colt said. "We've done our best."

Holly reached for his hand. "We *have* done our best but it's a simply bandage on a broken heart. She needs us but she needs her past more."

"Okay, so what do we do?" Daisy asked as she reached for the teacup, swirling the tea bag as she studied the brew inside.

"We have an honest discussion with her about what she wants." It hurt to even say the words. To think about losing her daughter all over again. She closed her eyes for a few seconds.

"Holly, we don't have to do this right now," Daisy said, objecting to the plan. "I can't imagine how you must feel. She's yours and I know you've always wanted her."

"I do want her, Daisy. But I also want her happy. I want her to come here when she's ready. Not because she *has* to."

"So we talk to her?" Daisy swiped at a tear that trickled down her cheek.

"We do." Holly picked up her cup and stood. "I have breakfast."

They gathered the tray, the coffee and sugar and the three of them walked up the steps and made their way to the kitchen. They found Dixie inside, making herself chocolate milk.

"There's the coffee," she said. "I was looking for that."

"You're too young to drink coffee," Colt growled.

She laughed at him, but the laughter soon faded as she looked from one adult to the other.

"Are you having breakfast with us?" Dixie asked Daisy as she sat down at the kitchen table. She stuck her finger in the apple butter for a taste and Holly moved the container away from her.

"I am. I have to get back to Broken Arrow," Daisy said. "But I'll be back at the end of the month."

"Is that when I go home?" Dixie asked.

The words struck sharp, piercing Holly to the core. She'd hoped that Dixie was beginning to think of Hope as her home. She had wanted her daughter more than she could put into words, and even if it was selfish, she wanted Dixie to choose her.

She turned away to the sink, needing something to do until she could gather her courage and blink away the tears that threatened to fall. She drew in a shuddery breath. Colt gave her a smile of encouragement.

Last night as she and Dixie had drifted off to sleep on the couch, Holly had prayed for her daughter, for their future, and that they would make the right choices for Dixie.

Right now she prayed for peace.

Daisy put a biscuit on a plate and handed it to Dixie. The girl took it and spooned apple butter over the top.

"Why are you all staring at me?" Dixie asked as she scooped up a bite. "Did I do something wrong?"

"You didn't do anything wrong," Holly assured her. "You're actually perfect. With an extra dose of spunk."

Daisy took a seat at the table, with Holly and Colt following, their chairs scraping on the hardwood floor. Dixie stopped eating and sat her fork on the plate with a clank.

"You're scaring me."

Holly looked to Colt, needing him to take the lead. He nodded but first he took off his hat and bowed his head just long enough for her to know he had prayed.

"Dixie, this is about the hardest thing I've ever had to do. Second hardest." His eyes filled with moisture that he blinked away.

"You all just need to say what you want to say," Dixie said, her voice sharp and the pitch high.

"We think that this whole guardianship agreement has been unfair to you," Colt told her. "As excited as we were to bring you here and spend time with you, we think it was unfair for the pressure to be put on you and we think it was unfair to move you here without giving you time to adjust to the idea."

Dixie took another bite of biscuit and apple butter and she chewed, acting as if nothing had been said, that none of this concerned her. Holly wanted to pull her close and make it all go away, all of the heartache, the confusion, the loss.

"Well," Dixie finally said, "I guess it hasn't been easy."

"We want you to be able to do what feels best to you," Holly told her daughter. "We know that none of this is easy but we want you to feel free to tell us what you'd like to do."

"Like right now, or at the end of the month?" Dixie bit down on her lip and a tear trickled down her cheek. She looked at Holly with hurt filling her gray eyes. "You don't want me?"

"Oh, Dixie, of course I want you. I want you so much. But more than that, I want you to be happy. I know you're trying to act happy but I know you're still sad sometimes. And that's okay, too."

As they talked, Cooter came into the room. He eyed the humans and went directly to Dixie, practically crawling into her lap until she put her arms around his neck and pulled him close.

"So it's all up to me?" Dixie said, drying her eyes.

"Pretty much." Holly looked from her daughter to Daisy. "I think we all want you to know that we love you and that no matter what, we will continue to love you and be here for you. But for right now, we want to know that you're happy and whatever you choose, we'll work things out."

Dixie buried her face in Cooter's scruffy neck. "I don't want to make you sad." She peeked up at Holly. "But I think I want to go home with Aunt Daisy. I miss my stuff and my friends. I miss my school."

With those words, Holly's heart broke. Dixie pushed Cooter out of her lap, got up from her seat, and crawled into Holly's lap, wrapping her arms around Holly's neck.

"I won't be gone forever. I promise. I just want to go home for a little while."

"She can come back as soon as school is out," Daisy suggested.

Holly whispered into Dixie's hair. "If you want, I'll come see you."

"I want you to come see me," Dixie said. "And Dad, too."

"I'll be there," Colt assure her. "And we'll be here whenever you want us, whenever you want to come back."

Holly shot him a look, wondering about that statement. She would be here. She would always be here. But Colt had never planned to stay. Two days ago she'd heard him discussing a clowning gig that he couldn't miss.

It was wrong to give Dixie false hope like that. Wasn't it?

* * *

"When do we leave?" Dixie asked Colt's sister.

Daisy gave them all an apologetic look. "I didn't know we were going to do this or I would have made different arrangements. I planned on leaving today."

"Today?" Colt pushed back from the chair and stood up, walking to the window, trying to get hold of himself.

They were doing this for Dixie. But he had to wonder if this was the worst idea ever. Yeah, his sister had grown up but she was still his little sister. And now he was entrusting his daughter to her?

"Colt." Holly said his name, drawing him back. "We agreed."

"I know. I know that this is the right thing for Dixie. I just didn't expect it this soon, or..." He shook his head. He wouldn't give voice to his own pain, in case it hurt Dixie or made her change her mind for his sake.

"I don't have to go." She looked down at the empty plate. "I mean, it isn't bad here. I love you guys. And I love my family. And Grandpa Jack. I don't have to go."

"But you just said you *want* to go," Holly told her. She held Dixie in her lap, stroking her hair and telling her it would be okay. "I want you to be able to go home and see your friends. You need to have time to adjust to everything. And in time we will figure this all out."

"I want to go home," Dixie sobbed into Holly's shoulder. "For a little while."

"You take all the time you need," Holly told her.

Daisy got up and walked away from the table and Colt knew that this wasn't easy for her. As much as his sister loved Dixie, he knew she didn't want to pull her away from them.

Nothing about this situation was easy but Colt felt a sense of hope, that someday soon it would get easier. They would all heal and life would find a path that made sense. God would get them where they needed to be if they just gave Him the time to get them there.

"I'll come see you when I'm in Tulsa," Colt told his daughter. "If you want."

She looked up from where she rested on Holly's shoulder. "Why will you be in Tulsa?"

"I got a call, asking me if I could fill in for a friend." He hadn't meant to tell them this way but once he'd mentioned visiting her, he had to push on and tell the truth. "And I have another commitment coming up. It's all kind of sudden, but I'll make sure we get to see each other."

He gave Holly a look, silently pleading with her to understand. She didn't. Of course she didn't. She was losing her daughter—and him.

He'd definitely made a mess of things this time.

"I guess I should pack." Dixie slid from Holly's lap but kept Cooter close. "And I can take Cooter?"

Daisy nodded. "You can take Cooter."

Dixie stopped mid-stride. "What about my horse? What about Flash?"

"I'll take care of him," Holly told her. "And if you stay at Daisy's, we'll make sure he gets to you. If Daisy knows where we can board him."

"I have a few acres. He'll be welcome at my place." Daisy rubbed Dixie's back. "This can all change, according to what you want."

"Okay." Dixie glanced back at Holly. "Will you help me pack?"

"Of course."

And just like that, she was leaving, choosing her own path. Colt held it together until he got out the back door and across the lawn to the barn. Then he had a long talk with God about the unfairness of it. He shed a few tears in the process, then he walked away, knowing that they'd done the right thing. Unfortunately that didn't make it feel any better.

When it was time for Dixie and Daisy to leave, he stood at the car with them. They hugged until they were all in tears and Dixie appeared to be exhausted. He opened the door and put her in the car, making sure she had her seat belt on. With a final kiss on the top of her head he told her he loved her.

Holly followed and she held it together, smiling the entire time.

"It will be so good for you to see your friends and to finish the year at your school." Holly kissed her cheek. "And we'll go shopping. I haven't been to Tulsa in ages."

"I'll be back, I promise," Dixie said.

"I know you will." Holly gave her a final hug. "Be safe and call us when you get home."

She backed away, smiling the entire time Daisy's car went down the drive to the road. And then she crumpled to the ground and sobbed.

Colt reached for her, wanting to comfort her, to pull her to her feet.

"Go away, Colt."

"I can't leave you like this."

"Go." She stood, brushing herself off, tears still streaming down her cheeks. "I need for you to go now. You have places to be. I have a life to live."

"I'm here, Holly. I'm not going anywhere."

"But you are. When were you going to tell me?"

"I don't know. To be honest, I put it off because I knew that you wouldn't understand. I knew you wouldn't trust me."

She didn't respond, too exhausted from the fight and from saying goodbye to Dixie.

"Holly, someday I hope you'll realize that I'm a man you can trust." He stood in the yard, ten feet from her, knowing she might not even be hearing what he had to say to her. "Leaving doesn't mean I won't come back or that there is someone else. I love you. I've loved you almost my entire life. I know I've hurt you. I've let you down. I can't even imagine why you would trust me, but I want it. I want to be the man who deserves your love because I think your love, next to God, is the most precious gift I could ever have. If you ever decide to give me that gift, I won't misuse it. But first, you have to give me your trust."

She shook her head. "Not today, Colt. Today I can't even trust myself. I hurt so much that I can't have this conversation with you. It's like reliving Dixie's birth and feeling the pain all over again."

"I know," he told her. "I lived that day, too. You weren't alone."

"I was alone," she accused.

He looked down at his boots. "Yes, you were. But today you don't have to be."

She wiped away the tears rolling down her cheeks. Tears that just wouldn't stop. "I'm sorry but I can't do this. Not right now."

She turned away and walked up the steps to the house and he let her go because he understood. He needed some time, too.

The last thing he wanted was to lose her again. He didn't know how to keep her, how to win her. He headed to his truck and with a last look at her house, he drove away.

Chapter Fifteen

Holly slipped between crowded tables at the café, refilling coffee and water for her customers as Stacy wandered through the room delivering orders. Jess, who had become a well-trained waitress in Holly's absence, hurried through the dining room making sure her tables were taken care of.

It seemed Colt knew how to manage a diner. He also knew how to make it grow. In just a matter of weeks he'd added items to the menu, taught Jim a few lessons by using the internet and streamlined their ordering process. There were electronic monitors where there had once been an ancient cash register and he'd ordered a dishwasher and a flame grill.

She didn't appreciate the changes. Well,

maybe she did a little but she didn't want to. She didn't want the improvements to be because of him.

As she poured a cup of coffee, a screech interrupted her thoughts.

"Good grief, Holly, are you mooning over that man or what? You just poured coffee on my hand. Give a guy a warning if you're going to pour hot coffee on him, will ya?" Chet jerked back, reaching for his ice water and dousing his napkin in it to apply to his scalded hand.

"Chet, I'm so sorry. And no, I'm not mooning. That's just rude."

"Rude is burning a guy with coffee. The last time I seen you so distracted was the day he walked through the door. Now you're at it again and he's just been gone a few days." Chet grabbed the towel from her tray and sopped up the mess on the table.

"I'll do that, Chet. And your lunch is on me." She took the towel back and finished cleaning up the mess. "I really am sorry."

"Don't you worry about it." Chet patted her arm in a fatherly way. "I know this has been a tough week for you."

"Thank you, Chet." And then she had to hightail it out of the dining room before she started to cry in front of her customers. As she ran, she heard someone tell Chet it was his fault she was crying, that he should learn to keep his mouth shut.

As she went through the door of the kitchen, Stacy caught her shoulders so they wouldn't collide. "Boss, you okay?"

She nodded. "Good. Right as rain. I'm going to step outside for a minute."

"That's fine. I've got this covered." Stacy headed on through the door and Holly did a U-turn and headed for the back door of the café.

The air outside was warm after being in the cool interior of the café. She leaned up against the wall and breathed deep, closing her eyes for a moment to pray for peace. They'd done the right thing for Dixie. They had. She knew it.

"Working on your summer tan?" The voice came from the sidewalk. She opened her eyes and smiled at Rebecca.

"Yes. I'm determined to get one this year."

Rebecca eyed the steps that led to Holly. The building had once been an old store and on the side was a huge concrete loading dock. She thought that someday she might put chairs and string lights for evening dining.

Maybe add a roof. None of that really mattered at the moment but her brain seemed to wander more these days.

"Come on up," Holly told Rebecca.

The other woman came up the steps with effort. "Wow, those five steps feel like mountain climbing."

"I'm sure they do. I wish I could offer you a seat."

"No need, I'm meeting Isaac for lunch." She glanced at her phone. "He won't be here for ten minutes or so."

"So you're all ears?"

Rebecca nodded. "Something like that."

Holly shrugged. "What can I say, I feel a little bit like a snow globe at this point. I thought I was all settled in my life and then everything got shaken. Just as things settled again, another shake-up. I'm trying to have faith. Trust in the Lord with all your heart, right? I'm holding on to the part where it says He will direct my paths. But this path seems to have a lot of potholes."

"I know and I'm sorry." Rebecca leaned against the wall next to her. "It's been a rough couple of months for you."

"It has." She breathed, finding it easier now

to let her friends in. "But I've realized something about myself."

"What is that?" Rebecca grimaced and a hand when to her belly. "Whoa!"

"Did you just have a contraction?"

"Maybe. But carry on. Tell me what you've realized about yourself, I need a distraction."

"I don't think this is the time for my stories, Rebecca," Holly responded.

"Oh, it is. I assure you."

"Okay, I've realized I've closed myself off from friendships. I have them, just kept them at arm's length. My life has always been messy and it was easier to not let people in. And now I seem to be making up for that, don't I?"

"I'm glad you are," Rebecca said.

"Colt told me I needed to learn to trust. He's right. I need to trust him. And I've struggled with that. I've held our past over his head. No matter what he did for me, the past was there. The heartache was front and center."

"Remember the story of the prodigal?" Rebecca asked. "When he came home broken and broke, after using up everything he'd been given, the father brought him in and not only forgave him, but threw a party."

"Forgiveness."

"Mercy," Rebecca responded. "It's a hard lesson. It shows God's compassionate and unfailing love for us. No matter what, if we're willing to come to him, broken and humble, He will restore us. As humans it's a little more difficult to give that forgiveness to someone who has hurt us."

"I miss him," she admitted to her friend.

"And Dixie?"

She smiled at the mention of her daughter. "I miss her so much it's like a giant hole in my heart. We talk every night on the phone, and she's full of stories about her school and her friends. Cooter is learning new tricks. Her artwork is being featured in the school art show."

"Why don't you go?"

"Maybe." Holly hadn't thought about it. She'd been trying to give Dixie space.

"If she told you about it, I can almost guarantee she wants you there."

"You're right, I should go." She thought about Colt being in Tulsa at a buck-off. The art show would take place on Friday and the buck-off on Saturday. Isaac had told her the buck-off was a fundraiser for a bull-riding friend of Colt's with a sick child.

"You won't be sorry," Rebecca told her. "It's hard to give a part of yourself that can be shattered if the trust isn't earned. Isaac taught me to trust again. He made it impossible to not fall in love." At this she smiled sweetly. "I honestly planned to never marry, not after the disaster I made of my life with Allie's father. I think we have a lot in common. We were young and we made mistakes. Those mistakes changed our lives. This is why I teach the girls in my teen class at church to wait, because there is nothing fun about being a teenager with a baby. The repercussions are far reaching. Kids don't think about things like custody, or how expensive it is to provide for a baby."

Holly reached for her friend, giving her a gentle hug. "Rebecca, I am so glad you came to Hope to start your new life. But I'm going to take you inside now. You need to see your wonderful husband."

"Plus I think I'm going to have a baby now." Rebecca's grin started to change into a grimace.

"I think you are, too."

"And I think you are going to Tulsa," Rebecca said as they walked arm in arm back into the café.

"If you won't need me for anything, I think I'm going to see my mom and then I'm going to take off."

"I think you should go. I'm going to be busy for the next few days." Rebecca stiffened for a brief moment. "But when you get back, I think a casserole would be nice."

"It's a deal." Holly helped Rebecca to the dining room where they found Isaac, Carson and Jack.

"What's this?" Jack asked when he saw the two of them.

"I think we might need to skip lunch," Rebecca told her husband. "I think we might need to go to Grove."

Isaac and Carson were both on their feet. "I'm going to be a dad!" Isaac crowed.

"Did he just figure that out?" Carson asked Rebecca.

"He's kind of late to the party." Rebecca reached for her husband.

The West family departed the café. Holly's customers were cheering them on and wishing them all the best. She stood at the window, smiling as Isaac helped his wife into the truck. Carson hurried to his SUV with Jack, the soon-to-be grandfather. She smiled at the scene they created, the four of them.

She glanced back at her café, the place that had been her life for several years. She saw the changes wrought by a man who had shown her nothing but kindness, nothing but love, she realized. Everything Colt had done for her had been an act of love, even his bringing Dixie to her.

Her own brokenness had caused her to push him away. Today she didn't feel so broken. Today she felt loved—by friends, by her community and by God. Even from a distance, she felt His love.

Her thoughts turned back to Colt. She needed to find a way to show him how much his love meant to her. She wanted him to know that she loved him back. And as difficult as it had been for her to find trust, she trusted him.

Colt found his way to Dixie's art show, loving that his daughter had invited him. He'd seen her the day before and she'd told him that Holly would be there as well. When he'd found that out, he'd decided he wouldn't hold off making the trip back to Hope to see his new nephew, Jackson West. Colt loved that his brother had a son.

He'd like to have a son of his own someday.

The only problem was he had to figure out how to convince Holly to marry him. If she needed convincing, maybe they just weren't meant to be.

He wandered the room, searching for Dixie and Daisy, finally spotting them in a quiet corner. Dixie lit up when she saw him. He opened his arms and she ran to him.

"I'm so proud of you," he told her, swinging her around.

"Thank you. Now put me down. You're causing a scene." She squirmed in his arms and he put her down.

"You're a mess," he told her. "Is school out next week?"

"Yep."

He had hoped she'd say something about going back to Hope. She didn't. And he wasn't going to push. That's the deal he and Holly had made. When and if Dixie came home, it would be her decision. But they still had her in their lives and that was all that mattered.

When he reached the corner where the sixth-grade artwork was displayed, Daisy gave him a quick hug. "I hear we're the proud owners of a new nephew."

"We are. Jackson West."

"They named him after Dad." Daisy made a face. "I mean, that's fine, it's their baby."

"Forgiveness," Colt told her. "It's a healing thing."

"I like myself just fine, but thanks."

"Oh, hard heart, when will you have your comeuppance?"

"Why would I need a comeuppance?" she asked, truly offended. "I'm a good person. I live a good life."

"Yes, I know you are." Colt perused the art on the wall, finding his daughter's work. It was a charcoal drawing titled *Family*. Opal with her cat. Jack smiling, wearing a cowboy hat. Flash standing in the field. Cooter sitting next to Dixie. Becky, smiling down from heaven. It was a collage of people. He pointed them out to her, smiling as he realized the message she was sending. These were her people.

"I can't believe you can tell who they are!" Dixie hugged him tight.

"Of course I can tell. This is an amazing work of art."

"I'm going to hang it at my mom's house."

He teared up a little. "She'll love that. This is a special thing, Dixie."

"It felt special when I was drawing it. It's

all the generations of my family. And my animals."

"Yeah, I can see that. You've got talent, kid. I'm glad you came home, to Daisy. I'm glad you got to do this."

"Me, too." She stood at his side and he wanted her to always be there. He wanted to teach her to rope, to run barrels, to fish, to play fair, to lose. He wanted to be her dad, every single day. He wanted more than weekends, holidays and summers. He wanted it all.

And she deserved more. She deserved his very best. Holly deserved his very best.

He hadn't realized until Dixie showed up that he wasn't complete without her, without Holly. He'd just been skating through life with no anchor. They anchored him.

"Where's Holly?" he asked after a bit.

"She came and left," Daisy said rather noncommittally.

Had she left so she wouldn't have to bump into him?

"Is she already on her way back to Hope?" he asked.

"I guess," Daisy said with a shrug.

"You're a lot of help," he accused. "You were supposed to keep her here so I could talk to her."

"Shh, not in front of the child," Daisy half joked.

"I'm right here," Dixie countered.

This was getting him nowhere. The women in his life were a complicated bunch. He looked at the two standing near him and shook his head.

"You all are *not* helping," he repeated. "I'm trying to win her heart. I need to make sure she knows I'm coming back to Hope."

"Are you?" Dixie asked. "When?"

"Next week. I've decided I'm getting too old for bullfighting. Or maybe I just don't love it like I used to."

"You're going to quit?" Dixie's eyes widened.

"Yeah, I'm quitting. I'm going to raise some cattle, start a business I've been thinking about and hopefully get married."

Dixie hugged him tight. "I'm going to be your best man."

"You're eleven," he reminded her. "But first we have to catch us a bride."

"Good luck with that," Daisy mumbled.

"Thanks for the optimism."

"I'm just saying, this might not be as easy as you think. The two of you have more than a little water under the bridge. You're kind of gimpy, not exactly a great catch."

He tuned her out and focused on Dixie. She had a lot to tell him about school, her friends and about her visit with Holly. He heard all about their shopping trip, where they ate dinner, the clothes they bought and the new baby.

The more she talked, the more he felt his heart shifting, changing, wanting. If Holly hadn't left town, he would have been going after her, begging her to give him another chance.

Begging was probably not a good plan. When Holly became his, it would be by mutual agreement. She would come to him, ready to trust. Or she wouldn't come at all.

Chapter Sixteen

❧

Colt liked rodeo clowning. He enjoyed seeing the laughter, the smiles. He loved bringing people down from the stands, making
them a part of the show. It never failed to
make his day. He thought if he continued to
do anything with rodeo, it would be this.

Today he'd worn cutoff green pants with
suspenders, a worn pair of boots, a quilted
shirt and white makeup. Considering everyone these days had some strange aversion
to clowns, he kept the makeup light. He had
dark circles around his eyes, a couple of stars
near his eyes, big eyebrows that arched above
his eyes. Daisy had helped.

At the moment he stood on a barrel doing
that new dance as a bull named Kitty raced
around the arena.

"Colt, how's it going down there?" the MC asked. "You gonna try to hold that kitty?"

Colt shook his head and pantomimed being gored, holding his stomach and falling backward off the barrel, watching as Kitty spun in his direction. He yelled, "Uh-oh," and jumped in the barrel. Everyone laughed. He held tight as the barrel rolled, compliments of the one-ton kitty in the arena.

The MC, Mike Parker, laughed and asked if he was okay. He gave it a minute and then, as the music for a jack-in-the-box played, he managed to rock the barrel upright, one of his best tricks. He jumped, bouncing himself out of the barrel, and stood on the sides, swaying back and forth. Kitty turned to eye him.

"I think it's time for this kitty to go back in the cage," Mike said drily.

"I don't like that kitty cat," Colt said in his best Tweety Bird voice. "Bad, bad Kitty."

He saw his daughter sitting in the stands next to Daisy. Dixie was practically rolling. He loved the job more than ever now, because Dixie watched him.

"Hey, Colt, are your clowning days over?" Mike asked.

The question took Colt by surprise. Mike had no reason to ask him that. If he hadn't had the painted on brows, he's sure his own would have arched, and his eyes widened in surprise.

He shook his head and raised his hands. "Is this like a knock-knock joke?" he asked over his mic.

The crowd laughed and then they pointed.

"Sure looks like you've been replaced," Mike told him with a chuckle. "By a girl clown, no less."

Colt turned in the direction the crowd was looking. He saw all of his friends standing up back in the pens and on the chutes, watching the unexpected show. His heart began to pound because this clown in her patchwork outfit, her face painted up with a big smile and flashy, happy eyes, looked familiar.

He hopped over his barrel a few times, got it sideways and rolled it across the arena a few feet while standing on it, then he jumped down and bowed before his clown queen. As he stood, he had a trick up his sleeve, so to speak.

He pulled out the wand, waved it around and out popped the bouquet of flowers. He handed it over to his clown queen. She smelled them and hugged them and then stuffed them in the pocket of her clown pants so that the multicolored flowers were sticking up.

"Colt, have you met your replacement?" Mike asked, interrupting the moment. "Did the clown union send you notice that you're out? I mean, it's time we had a female clown. Don't you all think so?"

The crowd cheered. The clown—his very own Holly—turned in a circle, waving her arms in an outlandish way. The more she waved, the more the spectators cheered.

But Colt wanted her attention. She was here. With him. Why?

He turned, putting a hand to his heart. He wasn't going to talk to Mike the MC. He only wanted to talk to one person.

But she wasn't talking, she stood there staring at him with a painted-on smile. She backed up and he followed. She put a hand out, stopping him.

He tried to give her his imaginary heart, but she clearly already owned the real thing. She didn't need the invisible heart he held in his hands. He brought his hands back to his chest, reinstalling it.

"I don't think she's that into you, Colt," Mike teased.

He wanted to tell Mike to take a hike.

Holly made a pouty face and drew a line down her cheek, as if a tear were trickling. She reached for his face and did the same. And then she reached into her sleeve and pulled out a bright red handkerchief. Instead of handing it to him, she first pretended to blow her nose. She tried to hand it to him.

He shook his head.

She pulled back a little and shrugged. She pulled out another handkerchief, this one yellow. She looked at it, feigning surprise when it was attached to a blue handkerchief. She handed him the yellow one and kept pulling, handkerchief after handkerchief. As he gathered them up for her he wondered where this was all going.

He turned off the power to his headset.

"Holly?"

"Colt, are you talking to us? We can't hear you. Folks, can you hear Colt? Do you want to hear Colt?"

The crowd cheered. Colt ignored them. Holly ignored them. She gave him an imploring look with her dark eyes melting his heart.

She pulled the last few handkerchiefs from her sleeve and he noticed the last wasn't a handkerchief, it was paper. She grabbed it and he stood there, floored, unable to breathe as she went down on one knee in front of him, her eyes seeking his.

"Well, what do you know about that," Mike the MC spoke quietly. "I don't think Colt has been replaced. I think he's just been claimed. Sorry ladies, I think our handsome cowboy clown just got taken off the market."

"Yes," he whispered as he read the sign she held.

"MARRY ME" it read in bright red letters.

He turned on the power to his headset. "Yes," he repeated.

She turned the sign around and it read: "I love you."

He went down on one knee in front of her.

"I love you, too." Colt spoke softly but the cheering crowd heard.

Holly felt as if the world were spinning around her. She'd never been so frightened, so excited, so in love as she was at that moment. She remained on her one knee, aware of the crowds of people all around them. Aware that Dixie was in the stands, too.

Most of all, aware of the man who had just gone down on one knee in front of her. His silver-gray eyes caught and held hers. He took the sign from her hand and folded it up, putting it in his pocket, patting it.

"Yes," he repeated for all the world to hear.

"Yes?" she asked, stunned.

"You meant me, right?" he asked. "Because it's possible you got the wrong clown?"

"No, I got the right clown." She couldn't help but laugh. "It seems I'm a one-clown woman."

"That's good, because there is no other clown for me."

"I've missed you," she said. And then she wished the whole of Tulsa wasn't watching because she had so much to say. She wanted to tell him she trusted him. She loved him. She wanted to spend her life with him.

"I've missed you, too," he answered.

And then, in front of that stadium and the live broadcast, he kissed her. She put her arms around his neck and he lifted her off the ground. His lips left hers for a moment but then returned.

"Hey, Colt," Mike interrupted. "I think you've forgotten where you are."

Colt waved him away. He kissed her again and she started to laugh. She couldn't stop herself. This man of hers, she would never let him go.

"Folks, I think you've just witnessed the most romantic proposal I've personally seen. Let's give these two kids a big hand. Boys, could we show Colt an open gate out of the arena to escort his pretty clown fiancée? We've got a buck-off to finish up. And if you enjoyed that proposal, folks, share the love with our buddy Johnny and his family. They could use your support. Right, Colt?" Mike the MC spoke loudly, his show voice back in place. Holly waved, thanking him for taking part.

As they turned to depart the arena, a riderless horse entered with a makeshift wreath around its neck.

"Look at that, Colt, I think your friends are helping you out. Buddy, you can't let the woman be the only romantic one." Mike called out.

Colt caught the horse, a pretty gray, a ring of plastic roses around its neck. He swooped Holly up in his arms and placed her in the saddle. She smiled down at him, thankful for the lift from the arena. Her legs were shaky and her heart felt like it might break free and fly away.

"I love you," he said as he placed her in the saddle. "I have always loved you, even though I wasn't very good at showing it. I've let you down. I let Dixie down. From this day forward, I'm going to work at being the man you deserve. A man is to love his wife the way Christ loves the church," he said. "I do."

She leaned from the saddle and captured his lips in a kiss.

"I trust you."

They left the arena to the cheers of more than a thousand people who had witnessed the greatest proposal in rodeo history.

Epilogue

Two years later

Holly watched from the window of the house as her husband and daughter worked on Dixie's barrel-racing skills. She loved watching them together. She loved the bond that had grown as the weeks, months and now years had gone by.

They were a family. It had taken Dixie some time but she'd made a decision that first summer that she wanted to be with her parents full time. After all, she needed to help plan a wedding, be the best girl, and she hoped in time she'd be a big sister. Of course Daisy was still a very big part of her life, of their lives. Holly and Colt wouldn't want it any other way.

Colt worked with Holly at the café, but he

also trained horses. Together they'd bought an old Victorian house near the lake and they were remodeling it to be a bed-and-breakfast. Daisy gave them decorating advice from time to time but she was busy with her own life. That was another story…

Each Sunday they picked Opal up for church and brought her home for lunch. She was with them today, sitting in her chair, listening to her granddaughter shout as she made the barrels in her fastest time yet. There were moments she seemed to remember them and other moments she slipped further away, not even able to walk through the house without help. It was odd, but Holly found that her relationship with her mother had grown in the past two years. They'd cried together. They'd found peace. Today Holly had shared a secret with Opal. Maybe Opal understood, maybe she didn't, but she'd smiled as if she couldn't be happier. Even now she had a secretive smile on her face.

Her attention returned to the arena, to Colt. Her heart overflowed. After eighteen months of marriage, her life had never felt this complete. They were building something that would last a lifetime, for them and their children. She loved him more each day.

She left the house, walking across the yard to join them. Colt was focused on Dixie and he didn't turn to see her coming. She stopped at her mother's side and facing Opal, she put a finger to her lips. Opal giggled but she nodded.

"Cool him down," Colt said. She peeked to see where he was and she winked at Dixie. "Then you can brush him and grain him. Turn him out with Buster."

"Got it, Dad."

She dismounted, but she didn't lead the horse away. Instead she led him in circles, staying close to the fence.

"What's she up to?" Colt asked as he came up behind Holly. "Is there something going on that I should know about? Opal, are you okay?"

Opal giggled and Holly turned around, laughing as Colt jumped back, grabbing his heart. Dixie joined the laughter as she led the horse from the arena and joined them.

Colt looked from one to the other of them. "You've already proposed and as far as I remember, since we're definitely married, I accepted."

Holly made a face and Dixie giggled and pretended to sneeze. Holly pulled out one of her mystery red scarves.

"Not this again," Colt said, suspicious but

smiling. She wanted to kiss him but Dixie really didn't like PDA.

Holly pulled out another handkerchief and another.

"I hope there isn't something bad at the end of this." Colt stepped away, as if truly worried.

Opal clapped her hands and started to say something but Dixie stopped her. Holly handed Colt the handkerchiefs and he continued to pull each one free from the wide sleeve of her clown outfit.

At the end he tugged and nothing happened. She widened her eyes and nodded. He tugged a little harder and the final handkerchief popped out. Attached to it was a baby blanket, and attached to that, a tiny teddy bear.

The two items weren't new. She'd kept them a very long time. For over thirteen years they'd been hidden in a drawer in her room. From time to time she'd taken them out to sleep with, thinking of the baby girl who had been wrapped in that blanket. She'd cherished the pictures of herself and Colt with their infant daughter. Just recently she'd framed those pictures and put them on the mantel over the living room fireplace.

Colt stared at the object in his hands, then tears trickled down his cheeks. He handed the items to Opal and told her to take care of them, then he grabbed her up in a hug and held her tight.

"Grandma Opal and I should go unsaddle my horse." Dixie reached for Opal. "Come on, Grams, I think they need time alone."

"I love the baby," Opal said.

"I know." Dixie sounded a little watery as she said it. "Me, too. I'm going to be a big sister. You're going to be a grandma again."

Opal patted Dixie's hand. "I know."

They left, Opal carrying the stuffed animal and blanket, Dixie leading her horse.

"We're having a baby," Colt said with wonder. "We're going to have a baby."

He whooped and hollered and picked her up to swing her around. But then he stopped, settling her back on her feet with the gentleness of a mother with a newborn.

"Colt, I won't break."

"I know you won't but…it's a baby. We're having a baby."

"Yes, Colt, we are having a baby." She laughed, even though a few tears escaped to slide down her cheeks. Happy tears. The best kind.

"The bear," he said, struggling, it seemed, to compose himself.

"The very one," she answered. He'd bought it for her; it had been attached to flowers and a box of candy. It had upset her at the time. She was having a baby she couldn't keep. She hadn't wanted flowers or gifts. In hindsight it had been the sweetest gift he could have given her. It had been a memory.

He hugged her again, his lips settling on hers in a feather-soft touch. "I need to warn you now, I'm going to be overprotective. I might suffocate you with the need to take care of you. But I love you, so you'll forgive me. I'm making up for the time I wasn't there for you."

"This is now," she told him. "This is our family, Colt, and we're going to live this moment today, not in the past. I want to enjoy every moment of this pregnancy with you, with our daughter and our family."

"Agreed."

Together they walked back to the house, arm in arm. Cooter barked and rushed ahead of them.

* * * * *

If you loved this story,
pick up the other books
in the Mercy Ranch *series,*

Reunited with the Rancher
The Rancher's Christmas Match
Her Oklahoma Rancher
"His Christmas Family"
in Western Christmas Wishes
The Rancher's Holiday Hope

from bestselling author
Brenda Minton

Available now from Love Inspired!
Find more great reads at
www.LoveInspired.com

Dear Reader,

The Prodigal Cowboy was quite a journey for me because it was so different from many of my previous books. I hope you'll enjoy the difference.

Colt and Holly have a long history of friendship, love and heartache, but at the core of their relationship is the love they've always had for each other. Love should be simple but it is a complex emotion that includes the pasts of both people, their insecurities, their personal experiences and their ambitions. For Colt and Holly there is a lot of the past and not a lot of the present at the heart of their relationship. It is only when they begin to deal with their past hurts that they can move on to the present. And to the future. A future which may—or may not—include a special girl named Dixie.

Brenda Minton

COMING NEXT MONTH FROM
Love Inspired

Available May 19, 2020

HER AMISH SUITOR'S SECRET
Amish of Serenity Ridge • by Carrie Lighte
Recently deceived by her ex-fiancé, Amish restaurant owner Rose Allgyer
agrees to temporarily manage her uncle's lakeside cabins in Maine. Falling
in love again is the last thing she wants—until she meets groundskeeper
Caleb Miller. But when she discovers he's hiding something, can she ever trust
him with her heart?

THE NANNY'S AMISH FAMILY
Redemption's Amish Legacies • by Patricia Johns
Starting her new schoolteacher job, Patience Flaud didn't expect to help Amish
bachelor Thomas Wiebe with the *English* daughter he never knew existed. But
as she works with the child to settle her into the Amish way of life, Patience
can't help but be drawn to the handsome father and adorable little girl.

STARTING OVER IN TEXAS
Red Dog Ranch • by Jessica Keller
Returning to his family ranch is the fresh start widower Boone Jarrett and his
daughter need. But he quickly learns rodeo rider Violet Byrd will challenge his
every decision. Now they must find a way to put aside their differences to work
together...and possibly become a family.

THE COWBOY'S SACRIFICE
Double R Legacy • by Danica Favorite
Lawyer Ty Warner doesn't quite believe Rachel Henderson's story when the
single mother arrives at her long-lost grandfather's ranch. She's hoping he'll
connect her with family who might donate the kidney she needs to survive. But
when he learns she's telling the truth, he'll do anything to help her.

A MOTHER'S HOMECOMING
by Lisa Carter
Charmed by the two-year-old twins in her toddler tumbling class, Maggie Arledge
is shocked to learn they're the children she gave up for adoption. And now
sparks are flying between her and Bridger Hollingsworth, the uncle caring for the
boys. Can she let herself get attached...and risk exposing secrets from her past?

BUILDING A FAMILY
by Jennifer Slattery
Worried the reckless bull rider she once knew isn't the right person to care for
their orphaned niece and nephew, Kayla Fisher heads to her hometown to fight
for custody. But Noah Williams is a changed man—and he intends to prove it.
Might raising the children together be the perfect solution?

**LOOK FOR THESE AND OTHER LOVE INSPIRED BOOKS WHEREVER
BOOKS ARE SOLD, INCLUDING MOST BOOKSTORES, SUPERMARKETS,
DISCOUNT STORES AND DRUGSTORES.**

LICNM0520

ReaderService.com has a new look!

We have refreshed our website and
we want to share our new look with you.
Head over to ReaderService.com
and check it out!

On ReaderService.com, you can:

- Try 2 free books from any series
- Access risk-free special offers
- View your account history & manage payments
- Browse the latest Bonus Bucks catalog

Don't miss out!

If you want to stay up-to-date on the latest at the Reader Service and enjoy more Harlequin content, make sure you've signed up for our monthly News & Notes email newsletter. Sign up online at ReaderService.com.

RS19